HERE BE
GHOSTS

HERE BE GHOSTS

GERRY KENNEDY

THE O'BRIEN PRESS, DUBLIN.

O'BRIEN PRESS

First published 1980
The O'Brien Press
11 Clare Street Dublin 2

© Copyright 1980 Gerry Kennedy

All rights reserved. No part of this
book may be reproduced or utilised in
any form or by any means, electronic or
mechanical, including photocopying, recording
or by any information storage and retrieval
system without permission in writing
from the publisher.

ISBN 0 905140 78 8 Paperback
ISBN 0 905140 80 X Hardback

Jacket design — John Devlin
Jacket photo — David O'Hehir
Typesetting — Redsetter Ltd.
Printed in the Republic of Ireland
by Irish Elsevier Printers Ltd.

Published with the assistance of the Arts Council

Here be ghosts that I have raised this Christmastide, ghosts of dead men that have bequeathed a trust to us living men. Ghosts are troublesome things in a house or in a family as we knew even before Ibsen taught us. There is only one way to appease a ghost. You must do the thing it asks you. The ghosts of a nation sometimes ask very big things; and they must be appeased, whatever the cost...

P. H. PEARSE
from *Political Writings and Speeches*

1

ALL MY TROUBLES started in the ESB.

The Electricity Supply Board. Or, depending on one's linguistic affiliations. An Bord Solantais Electris. Or something. I'm not at all sure that my Irish spelling is what it should be. Particularly for a chap who spent, in remote childhood, a month in even remoter Donegal . . . learning the language from Native Speakers.

We lived on tomatoes.

I remember it well. Tomatoes. Breakfast, dinner and tea. Because, you see, in those far off days, there was a scheme afoot. A scheme which involved the building of glasshouses all over Donegal and suchlike deprived areas . . . thereby creating an industry. And an awful lot of tomatoes.

Which nobody wanted to eat.

So. They imported us, hundreds of linguistically deprived little buggers from Dublin. To eat the tomatoes. And learn Irish.

It didn't work.

People who live in glasshouses shouldn't try to kill two birds with one stone. It was a shambles. The first week I shared my bed with four other thirteen year old boys. This was due to some administrative difficulties and did nothing to further my knowledge of Irish. Though it did broaden my mind in other ways.

So.

The ESB. And my troubles. Which started there.

I was a Clerical Officer in Head Office. This position I had held down, much in the manner of a man dealing with an epileptic, for some eight years. Over these eight years I performed many important functions for The Board, chopping and changing. As one department got tired of me I was moved to another. And, at the time of which I write, I was in Public Relations, answering letters from cranks and people in iron lungs who were anxious about the possibility of power failure, that sort of stuff . . . chaps on kidney machines, they have worries too.

So. I was in Public Relations. Prior to which I'd been in Debtors, negotiating with recalcitrant payers, cutting them off when they got on my nerves, other times arranging that they pay so much a week to clear their arrears. These latter times, when I felt lenient, coinciding with sexual cycles of my wife Anna. This was a vital factor in my activities. At menstruation time the lights went out. And no damn nonsense about poverty or unemployment from the improvident buggers. There's no excuse for anyone to fall behind with their ESB bills, none whatsoever. Details of schemes many and various are available for the asking, savings stamps, bank drafts, all sorts of things. Leaflets are available describing these schemes. Leaflets with little pictures of fifty pence pieces to facilitate illiterates. We think of everything in the ESB.

But people won't learn.

My days were made a misery by old age pensioners weeping on the other side of my desk. The swine. They got on my nerves. What did they CARE . . . about me? Nothing, that's what they cared. And so, reasoning that most of them had been brought up in pre-electrification days anyway . . . well . . . it wouldn't do them much harm to go back to candleville for a while . . . now would it?

I cut them off ruthlessly.

Then what happened? WELL . . . the ESB decided to develop a human face. They were being pressurised by the media. Old folks were dying of the cold. Families were going without hot dinners. In short, people were paying the price for their inadequate way of arranging their affairs, as if that were our fault.

Hot dinners have nothing to do with accounting procedures.

That's exactly what I said when asked by the higher-ups to be a bit more lenient. They appreciated my position. But there are wheels within wheels. I was transferred to Public Relations.

And was I annoyed? Yes. I was furious.

I brooded. At my lunch hour. Sitting on a park bench in Stephen's Green I brooded, remembered, thought of lost opportunities, thrown away years; the whole life crisis bit.

I realised that I should have stayed in Insurance.

I'd been quite happy as a clerk in the Irish Life Insurance Company. The actuarial department. Actuarily. Quite happy. How foolish of me to have thrown all that up. Just for the added security that the ESB could offer a married man.

It was my mother-in-law's fault. It usually is.

She THOUGHT that the ESB would be a better bet for a long term career. One never knows, she said, one never knows what could happen to Insurance companies in the future. Insurance is subject to the whims of commercial life. Not so electricity.

One could not envisage a future without electricity.

I saw her point. Then. Ahh those heady days of eight years ago, economic expansion, Zen, Yen, hotpants, Conor Cruise O'Brien, glorious summers, the Big Wind, Mary Kenny waving contraceptives at railway employees, miniskirts, teargas-crazy RUC running wild . . . and Gay Byrne before the male menopause . . . aahh . . . those days . . . where are they now?

Gone.

And NOW I can envisage a future without electricity. Without oil. Or food. Or civilisation. Or, indeed, without anything. I am a gloomy man. The news is bad. Soon I must away to the hills with me and mine, some heavy weaponry for our protection . . . and a sack of seed potatoes on my back.

BUT . . . eight years ago I was an optimist. Eight years ago I didn't want to do anything that might upset my future mother-in-law. Particularly when her daughter's breasts were shortly to be mine. I was a breast fetishist. Still am. Not one of these characters who change their fetishisms like dirty socks. I wear mine continuously. Some things are sacred. Though once in my foolishness I went along to a lady psychiatrist in Fitzwilliam Square to see if she could do anything for me. She couldn't. Not a bit of it. Her chest was as flat as her clipboard.

So. Eight years ago, to keep the mother-in-law happy, to get hold of her daughter's breasts, eight years ago I would have . . . would have . . . would have gone to work in Bord na Mona, the turf board, that Gulag Archipelago of the bureaucratic world. Sex can be a fearful task master.

Any old how. I went to the ESB and stayed there eight years. Eight years of loyal and dedicated service. Mostly to myself, I admit, but loyal and dedicated service nonetheless. And NOW, for my pains, I was to be transferred to Public Relations. And that was that.

I sat on my park bench and shrugged. That was that and maybe it was a good thing. A blessing in disguise. An ill wind that blows. A stitch in time. A dictionary of proverbs. Maybe it was . . .

Because . . .

The truth of the matter was that I hadn't really been getting on that well with my colleagues in Debtors. Not to put too fine a point on it . . . no-one was talking to me. Because of the situation in the Philippines.

To elaborate . . .

At the time of which I write there was some controversy among us clerical chaps about whether we should DEMAND that our employers, the ESB, demand that they cease and forthwith too from supporting the tyrannical and oppressive regime in the Philippines by providing them with electrical expertise.

Some controversy indeed.

Meetings were held. Motions were passed. Directives were issued. Sub-committees were formed. Spokesmen were appointed and instructed to pass on views. Yes. The place was a hotbed of agitation. Marxists came out from behind filing cabinets. Teagirls had their say. I had my say.

This made me unpopular.

My say usually makes me unpopular. Because I am DIAMETRICALLY opposed. Always. My basic philosophy being that the mob are invariably wrong and when the mob moves in one direction, I speed off in the opposite.

I am an individualist.

An unpopular individualist. So. On my park bench, I shrugged. It was just as well. All for the best. The die was cast. I vacated my bench . . . went back to work.

Not without a tinge of sadness. As I cleared out my desk. Transferred my potted plants. Took one last look at the bottom of the typist . . . goodbye . . .

* * *

Officially, I was to quote deal with complaints and queries from the general public unquote. Sounds easy enough. BUT . . . as the weeks went by I realised that all the letters from CRANKS were being directed to my desk. Interesting? Yes, certainly. But worrying too. Had, I brooded, had the higher-ups decided in their wisdom that I was a crank too? And were they operating on that 'set a thief to catch a thief' system?

Perhaps . . . perhaps they were.

But nothing could be done about it. If they wanted me to deal with cranks . . . then that is precisely what I would do . . .

I have always had a positive approach to life.

And cranks are interesting. There are people out there that think electricity is a form of magic which is affecting their hormonal secretions, their hair growth, sex-life, geraniums.

WORRIED people . . .

Interesting people. My kind of people. I began to enjoy the work, lashing out letters to places like Sneem. And Ballaghderreen, both towns inordinately over-populated with cranks. People suffering from sex-changes since their house was re-wired, that sort of stuff.

O ICed you not . . .

On my files I had correspondence with a retired clergyman who was changing sex since his grateful parishioners gave him a present of a colour TV as a going-away present.

He felt it was the rays emitted. And what did I think?

Dear Reverend . . . . . . (Name deleted),

Further to yours of the sixteenth ultimo, I have been in touch with our technico-medico department who will shortly be sending me their report on your problem. In the meantime please find enclosed a Gossard Wonderbra which I am sure will alleviate your discomfort. The price of this article will be added to your account in the normal manner.

Mise le meas,
Martin O'Shea
(Consumer Information Dept.)

That's what I thought.

And that's the sort of letter I wrote in reply to my cranks. Not that I posted them, oh no, I wrote them to amuse myself, to while away the weary hours. The letters that actually got posted were a totally different kettle of fish. Bland, non-committal, carefully screened by the Legal Department in case we put our foot in it and ended up in the High Court.

A place most desirable to stay out of.

2

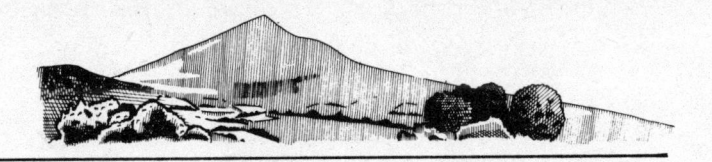

MONDAY THE SIXTEENTH of June was much the same as any other day. I got up, kicked the bedroom chair, looked at my wife's breasts as she dressed and thought . . .

How the mighty have fallen.

I smiled at the little pun, breakfasted lightly and then, still smiling, I emerged from my modest little semi in Glenageary, my modest little daughter Aoife at my side. I escorted her to nursery school. (Montessori with a hint of Froebal). My wife would collect her later. We were careful parents. There are perverts about, even in Glenageary. They lurk in hedges, just waiting to leap out upon unescorted seven year old daughters of ESB clerical officers . . .

Civilisation is a fragile thing. Man the BEAST is lurking. But I am careful. I'm not easily fooled by the polite *Good Morning* from my neighbour as I pass, little Aoife skittering by my side. I'm not easily fooled. Because I KNOW. I KNOW that that very same neighbour, who, incidentally, works for An Foras Taluntais in an unspecified capacity, as indeed do most workers in the Forases . . . I know that too.

I know that my neighbour is only WAITING. For the opportunity. To ravage my little pre-pubescent Aoife. It's the beast in him. He can't help it. He's not to be blamed. Merely watched. So I watched him. Suspiciously.

Then, Aoife safe at nursery school, I walked to the station, carefully trying not to think of my feet. If I start thinking about my feet, when I'm walking, I fall over. Well . . . not REALLY fall over, I develop the FEAR of falling over. Walking is more complex than the average man realises.

And I am not the average man.

Though I probably looked it, standing on the station platform with my fellow commuters, waiting, watching . . .

the sky . . . the once elegant no doubt brick and terra-cotta of the station buildings and how they were falling to bits through years of long neglect and the rise of trade unionism.

Where (I asked myself) . . . where are the pretty flower beds now? The well raked gravel. The white washed stones. The porters who wore uniforms and had a proper respect for the passengers who after-all-and-let's-not-forget-it . . . dammit . . . who are paying the buggers' wages. Where are they now?

Indeed. Where ARE they now? And where are the trains now, more to the point. . . . where are the trains, I thought, as, shifting from one hand-stitched Italian slip-on to the other, I watched the lights flickering meaningfully from red to green. And back again. Some deranged signalman in Claremorris Junction a hundred miles away obviously pressing millions of pounds worth of electronic buttons with great gusto, drunk with High Technology, totally oblivious to real things. Like the ACTUAL arrival of an ACTUAL train at my platform.

HAH. I said. Grumpily looking across the tracks. On the opposite platform a gaggle of green-uniformed schoolgirls with all the impedimenta of their trade. Schoolbags, luncheon kits, hockey sticks, fat little breasts in blouses and long legs dangling from the hems of short green skirts.

HAH. I said. To myself. Those schoolgirls are on their way to that expensive convent in Killiney. Their daddies are rich, publicans, ambassadors, solicitors, night club owners and suchlike, rich. And I am not. It is sad. Life is sad. Rich people are sad. Poor people are sad. We are all sad. Stations are sad places. The coming . . . and the going. Sad. Schoolgirls are sad. Their long slender legs and the glimpses of firm young thighs firm young thighs firm young . . . are very sad too.

HAH. I glared across the railway tracks. To be or not to be. (Hamlet). To hurl myself across the tracks and have my way with them. Or to stay here, wait patiently for my train like a good citizen. To be or not . . . the old question. Good old Shakespeare. (Incidentally he was Irish). To be or not . . .

It'd be so EASY to clamber across the tracks to the firm breasted ones . . . though with my luck I'd be mincemeated by an express thundering unexpectedly on its way to the Wexford Opera Festival with its load of Leading Citizens in monkey suits and their womenfolk in décolletage . . . diamonds dangling in the wrinkled folds of their withered dugs. HAH.

And still no train. And me getting angrier by the minute. By the second. Reaching such a pitch of anger and rage that I began to lose interest in the dozens of firm young breasts opposite, and that's ANGRY . . . then the rumour came, whispering among my fellow commuters . . . someone has killed himself in Dalkey, the station down the line. I wasn't surprised. Dalkey is a bistro of boutiques, a pot-pourri of après-ski, a place of scrawney shanked housewives with thin lips, pot-bellied husbands on day leave from the coronary care centre, BMWs, restaurants with low lights and high prices . . . I wasn't surprised that someone had thrown himself in front of a train in Dalkey . . but who could it have been? One of the eminent residents, Hugh Leonard the playwright perhaps? Hardly. No. Much more likely to have been an unknown little anonymous person like myself. One of the teeming millions whose deeds go unsung, who lives his drab life quietly to the best of his ability, preserving some of the old values, carrying on the heritage of plod to the next generation. Yes.

But anyway. The train wasn't going to come and we'd all have to go by bus and like it or lump it and that's what we did, streaming out of the station like lemmings, tut-tutting among ourselves. And so and so and so . . . as the filthy semi-derelict omnibus carried me unwillingly into the city I thought

Sure it's all for the best.

Sure it would've been terrible anyway to have been run over by the Wexford Opera Special whilst trying to clamber across to the firm young breasts. Death at the wheels of a trainload of tone deaf social climbers is no fitting end for anyone. Least of all a Clerical Officer in The Electricity Supply Board.

* * *

Tired and late and fed-up, but alive, I arrived at work, muttering curses and foul oaths between my clenched lips. I was so late, in fact, that I missed the early morning tea-break . . .

My day was ruined

Before it began.

I looked at the pile of letters from cranks that awaited me in my in-tray. And the first one I opened was totally absurd. This bugger had bought a washing machine on tick and now, he alleged, it was walking across the floor like a dalek suffering from the vibrations. Not only that, it was CHEWING up the washing like a goat. Not only THAT . . . it was WATCHING HIS WIFE'S BOTTOM . . . as she bustled about the kitchen.

HAH. (I said). This man is not a CRANK. This man is MAD. This is a chucklehead. A banana. Pathological, psychotic and, most likely, PARANOID too. A monkey nut.

He lived in Griffith Avenue. That figured. We get a lot of lulus in Griffith Avenue. I know how to deal with that lot. No better man. I picked up my bic, and wrote . . . (in a fine, educated hand) . . .

> *A Chara,*
> *With reference to your letter of the fourteenth inst., I am instructed to inform you that the beauty of the world hath made me sad, this beauty that will pass. And while mostly our washing machines give complete satisfaction, sometimes they don't. Life is like that. Full of sometimes. Sometimes my heart hath shaken with great joy, to see a leaping squirrel in a tree, or a red ladybird upon a stalk. Or little wabbits in a field at evening, lit by a slanting sun, dying of mixupmytosis. Or children with bare feet upon the sands of some ebbed sea, or playing in the streets off Griffith Avenue. Things young and happy. Things like a man with a perfect washing machine.*
> *AND THEN my heart hath told me: These will pass, will pass and change, will die and be no more. Things bright and green, things young and happy. And I have gone my way. Sorrowful.*
> *Mise le meas,*
P. Pearse.

I put this letter, not in my out tray, no, but in the pile of letters that had come back cleared from the legal department, letters waiting to be put in envelopes prior to posting.

Why did I do such a foolish thing?

Because sick and tired I was. Sick and tired. Sick and tired of pandering to bananas in Griffith Avenue. I'd show the buggers. I was not to be trifled with ...

I HAD FEELINGS TOO.

Deep down, a man is just a man. Sooner or later a man's got to kick out for the surface of the swimming pool of crap (which is LIFE) in which he flounders, breathe in the fresh air of freedom, do what he likes ... NAY ... do what he MUST ... which I did ... and it pleased me immensely.

And the day passed pleasantly afterwards. In the lift one of the typists from the second floor brushed against me, her nipple to my elbow. And I am sure it was a deliberate gesture.

All is not lost.

There's life in the old dog yet.

Thirty-two is not OLD ... for Jesus' sake ... now is it?

* * *

That very evening my wife and I went to see 'Pinnochio' in the local cinema. We had ice creams too. And, later, taking the babysitter home in my Allegro, the girl deliberately exposed large areas of thighs to my gaze. The brat.

It had to be DELIBERATE, didn't it?

I don't know what the younger generation is coming to.

That's what I thought. As I rushed home to the wife. Whereupon, it never rains but it pours, she took it upon herself to make love in the female superior position, her large floppy breasts swinging about wildly and bashing me about the ears in an agreeable manner.

All in all, A GOOD DAY.

3

ON THE TWENTY-FIRST day of June I was summoned to the office of my superior.

'Have you gone MAD, Mr O'Shea?' he asked.

'Not that I know of, sir', I replied, carefully keeping all the options open.

'Humph', he said, looking at me carefully. And then, picking a letter off his desk, he began to read. The first few sentences brought it all back. It was mine of the sixteenth inst., to the chap in Griffith Avenue, the washing machine man . . .

Well . . . hearing it re-read like that . . . welll . . . it certainly did sound eccentric, I had to admit. So I admitted. And my superior harumphed again, picked up a second letter from the desk. This one he had received from the outraged consumer. (We, in the ESB, always refer to the customer as 'Consumer'; just a little thing of ours.)

Well apparently this outraged consumer was a second cousin to a TD or some damn thing or other, (aren't we all?), but this bugger alleged in no uncertain terms that we had not heard the last of the matter . . . not by any manner of means NO. HE wasn't going to be pushed around by bureaucrats and if a new washing machine wasn't on his doorstep forthwith then the Sunday World would want to know the reason why . . . and more, much more of that ilk . . .

I shrugged.

My superior put the letter down.

Then HE shrugged.

We get a lot of letters like that in the ESB.

We shrug a lot too. If you've ever noticed, all us clerical chaps pouring out into Fitzwilliam Street of a lunch hour, ever noticed our humped shoulders . . . well . . . we get that from shrugging. It's an occupational hazard. Like asbestososis. What one gets in brake-lining factories. Or silicosis, in mines . . . but enough of social awareness.

I felt I should do a little explaining. My superior obviously felt likewise. He looked at me expectantly.

'I've been under strain', I murmured.

My superior cocked his head to one side, in the 'oh yes?' position. My explanation obviously needed enlarging.

'The wife has had a hysterectomy'.

This got him where it hurts. He leaped back in his seat, looking shocked. Also looking thoughtful, obviously trying to work out which part of the female anatomy was involved in hysterectomy work. I stared at him. After about half a minute he started to massage, absentmindedly, his left chest with his right fist.

He'd reached the wrong conclusion. No Greek in the man.

'Well I'm sorry to hear that, Mr O'Shea . . . but really . . .' he waved the offending letters in the air . . . 'maybe you'd like to take some leave?'

'Well I'm saving up my leave for a boating holiday on the Shannon. We're renting a cruiser from the Emerald Star line. It's the holiday of a lifetime.'

'It certainly is. If it doesn't rain.'

'Oh I don't think it will rain', I said, airily, waving a well-manicured hand through the air.

'How can you be so sure?'

'Well I can't be SURE . . . of course I can't be SURE . . . but I sort of feel that it definitely won't rain. My friend Walter feels that too.'

'Walter?'

'Yes. Walter and Susan, our friends, they're sharing the boating holiday. They have a little boy. Live three doors up. On our estate.'

'I see.' He looked at me thoughtfully.

I looked at him, wondering if he really did SEE. Could he read my mind? Could he tell that my friend Walter and I had carefully arranged this boating holiday, in Fitzgerald's Public House in Sandycove for the purpose of screwing each other's wives?

AH HAH. The plot thickens . . .

Not that each other's wives knew about this arrangement YET. All in good time. We felt, my friend Walter and I, we felt that the Shannon would be a suitable ambience for wife-swapping. The watery wastes all around, the undressing in confined spaces, the investment in a couple of bottles of vodka . . . and Bob's our uncle.

We hoped.

'Well', (SAID MY SUPERIOR), 'well let's hope it doesn't rain. Anyway . . . you could always take some compassionate leave.'

'Compassionate? That's only for deaths . . .'

'A hysterectomy is quite serious.' He rubbed his chest again. 'Where did she have it?'

'Vincent's', I said, mentioning the name of the only Dublin hospital which hadn't been built for the wounded returning from Napoleonic wars. Only the best for my Anna.

'Expensive?'

'Voluntary Health Insurance. I have dozens of units.' I nodded smugly. 'Dozens.'

'Wise man. Wise man. You can't have too many units in the Voluntary Health. That's what I always say.'

'Right. You never know.'

'Never know what?'

'When you'll be struck down. I mean one day there you are . . . right as rain . . . and the next . . . lung cancer . . . you never know . . .'

I nodded wisely. As I always do when delivering pearls of my homespun wisdom about such matters as health, life, fate or the inherent limitations of existence. Wisely I nod. Often to myself. Like times I read in my Evening Press that yet another health freak has dropped dead while jogging. Or been run over by a juggernaut-ful of Common Market-bound butter . . . cholesterol saturated butter . . .

Aaah.

Aaaaah yes.

BUT. As I nodded, there in his office, my superior was unfortunately lighting yet another of his interminable cigarettes. At the mention of the dreaded word 'cancer', as it dropped from my lips like an aborted foetus might drop into the lap of Archbishop Dermot Ryan, i.e., unsuitably . . . as that happened my superior paused, looked at me strangely. For a moment. But it was a moment that put the chances of any promotion for me at least a year further away.

'Hmmm. Welll.' He shuffled papers. 'Hmmm. I really feel that a week off, a bit of rest, do you good. Stave off . . .' He waved my letter again . . . 'Stave off what could be a nervous breakdown. Do you drink?'

'Not to excess,' I said as sharply as my hangover would allow me.

'Good. Drink is the divil.' Saying this he casually polished his pioneer pin with the tip of a finger. I felt some remark was called for.

'It must be difficult, keeping off it totally.'

'Never a drop has passed my lips', he mentioned.

'That's some achievement', I agreed, 'particularly these days'.

He tapped the side of his head significantly. 'Will power. That's all it takes. Will power.'

'And that's in short supply', I ventured, warming to this geriatric exchange of retired Indian Army colonels' views. 'In short supply. It's all easy-come-easy-go. These days. If it's not drink it's sex. Or drunken sex. Gang bangs in Ranelagh. State of affairs. Shocking. Grab the quick thrill. Live to-day. Never count the cost. God is a multiple orgasm. Life is . . .'

I paused for breath. My superior, grabbing the opportunity, held up his hand in a tired 'STOP' gesture. Like a traffic policeman suffering from lead poisoning. 'Yes, Mr O'Shea . . . but . . . as I said . . . a week off . . . do you good.'

I got the impression that he wanted my week off to start as soon as possible. So I stood up. To go. But where? So many places beckoned. Malibu. Bali. Torridmolinos. Kinsale where they have all those good restaurants run by refugees from Surrey. Where? The world was not merely my oyster . . . it was a veritable seafood extravaganza . . . a spanish paella complete with baby octupuses and their little legs dangling sickeningly over the edge of the plate as if trying to run away from me and Anna on our honeymoon.

Long ago in Spain.

Sunburn, sand and sea and sex. And all the sadness of wondering . . . where am I coming from . . . where will I go?

4

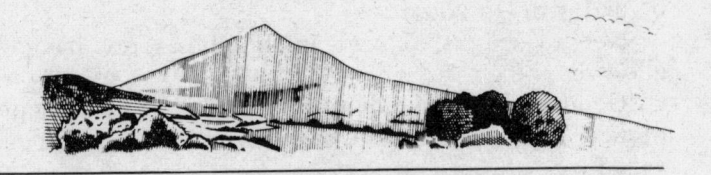

I WENT HOME. The suburbs were quiet and strange at that time of morning. The wife was still in bed, reading a paperback book and listening to the Gay Byrne Show on the radio.

'Aha,' I said, 'so this is how you spend your day you lazy slut.'

'Martin', she said, dropping the book into her cleavage, 'What are you doing home?'

'The ESB's gone bust. We're all laid off.'

'Don't be ridiculous. What are you doing HOME?'

I sat down on the bed and looked at her. She had blonde hair, blue eyes, big beautiful floppy breasts. I could quite well understand why my friend Walter wanted to get the wife-swapping business going. Why I wanted to was harder to discern. His wife was inordinately plain. And flat chested with it. But, I suppose . . . .

A change is as good as a breast . . .

'Martin', she removed the book from her cleavage, placed it to one side, then leaned over to the radio and turned down the Gay Byrne Show so that his voice became a ghostly thing, eerily whispering on about the problems of married men and young hussies in discotheques, 'MARTIN, WHAT ARE YOU DOING HERE AT THIS HOUR?'

'I'm on compassionate leave. Because of your hysterectomy.'

She sat up straight, open eyed. 'My WHAAA?'

'Hysterectomy', I murmured helplessly.

'I haven't had a hysterectomy . . . have you gone mad?'

'That's the second time I've been asked that question to-day.'

'I'm not surprised.' She reached out a hand, held one of mine. 'Come on, Martin, tell me . . . what's it all about?'

'WELL . . .' I took a deep breath, 'Well it all started with this letter from some eegit in Griffith Avenue. His washing machine was molesting his wife . . .'

'Don't be absurd.' She removed her hand from mine, looked at me sternly. I can't resist her stern look . . . So I reached out and grabbed one of those pendulous breasts of hers. And squeezed.

'MARTIN', she slapped my hand away, 'stop THAT.'

'Alright', I said. Putting my hand under the blankets and grabbing her by the thigh, subtly and simultaneously inserting my thumb into her vagina and revolving it in an anti-clockwise direction.

'MARTIN.'

'ANNA.'

'Don't Anna me. And stop THAT.'

'You're all wet and mucky. You've been masturbating again, haven't you?'

Anna giggled. Wiggled her hips. 'What if I have?'

'You'll go blind.'

'Buggery.'

'If you like.' I whipped away the blankets, rolled her over and leaped onto her back. ALL IN ONE SWIFT MOVEMENT . . .

AND THEN?

She wriggled out from under, grabbed me by the throat, punched me on the nose.

AND THEN?

I lost my temper. With a great primaeval ROAR I threw myself onto her, pummelled her into submission, tied her hands behind her back WITH ONE OF HER OWN NYLON STOCKINGS, tied her left ankle to the bedpost with ANOTHER OF HER OWN NYLON STOCKINGS, and, because she only had two legs, used her bra to tie her other ankle. To the other bedpost.

AND THEN?

Anna started to giggle.

'You're not meant to giggle,' I said, 'you're meant to beg for mercy.'

'Mercy schmercy', she squeaked.

WELL . . . two can play at that game. Now it just so happened, and I don't believe that I've mentioned this before, had no need to, really . . . but IT JUST SO HAPPENED that at this time in her life Anna was into making string lampshades.

SO?

So on the dressing table of our bedroom there was: a half finished string lampshade, a ball of string, some other impedimenta pertaining to the trade. She made these lampshades in bed. For her nerves.

HAH...

So. With a slow deliberate movement, I picked up the ball of string.

'What are you going to do?' she squeaked.

'You'll find out', I ominously replied.

She did. I tied the string around her right breast.

'That hurts', she objected.

'Life is pain and suffering', I mentioned.

'I'll get you for this', she threatened. 'And I'm cold. The least you could do is put a blanket over me. While you act out your pathetic fantasies.'

I pulled the string.

'EECH' she said.

I put a blanket over her, went downstairs, trailing the string, went into the kitchen, made a cup of coffee, sat down and read The Irish Times. Every so often, when the spirit moved me, pulling the string and listening for her 'EECH' upstairs. I turned on the downstairs radio, yes we're very posh, two radios... the G.B. show had now blended into something else. A man called Rodney Rice.

Contented, I sat there for some time.

AND THEN... I was reading the letters page of the paper, pulling the string absentmindedly... WHEN... something hard and heavy hit me on the back of the head.

A saucepan.

Anna had escaped. The clever bitch. Crept up on me, saying 'eech' at suitable intervals...

'Oh', I said, dizzy and dazed.

'Serves you right. SADIST.'

'You've given me a headache', I complained.

'Well you've given me a sore tit. So we're quits.' She massaged the offended mammary. 'Look at that, look at those bruises. You BRUTE.'

'There there, dear,' I murmured, 'I'll kiss it better.'

Well... one thing led to another... the way it does when an

attractive woman like Anna and an attractive man like me have a choice between listening to Rodney Rice on the radio or sex. I mean to say . . . well . . . anyway . . .

It was on the kitchen table, in a scatter of Irish Times pages, Anna's buttocks bouncing up and down on the leading article which, if I recall, pertained that day to the intractable problems of Namibia . . . it was there that we were copulating in the missionary position when the back door opened and someone screamed . . .

It was mother-in-law.

'Oh GOD', said Anna, closing both her eyes and her legs as tight as she could.

'Oh GOD', said me, burying my face in her hair.

'WELL', said mother-in-law, 'WELL . . .'

Well indeed. After that the morning went downhill. In fact it went so far downhill that it fell off the edge and vanished into merciful oblivion.

5

AFTER LUNCH I cut the grass. And it was while I was cutting the grass that I got an intimation that I was not psychically alone.

'Martin,' said a little voice in my head, 'I think it'd be better if you cut the grass crossways, so that the stripes go across the garden rather than longitudinally.'

'Well,' I replied, 'it's my bloody grass and I want the stripes longways. I always have my stripes longways. It's the right and proper thing.' And then I stopped in amazement. WHO WAS I TALKING TO?

'Who am I talking to?' I asked.

'Patrick Pearse', the voice replied.

'Patrick Pearse?? Patrick Pearse??' I staggered back in surprise. Up to then I had always believed that the Great Revolutionary Leader had been executed in 1916 and was safely dead and buried and not likely to further interfere with the Onward March of Progress. My knuckles whitened on the handles of the lawnmower. 'Patrick Pearse? Patrick Pearse is dead.'

'Stuff and nonsense,' the reply came, 'nobody's dead. Death is a concept which, outside the context of mortality, has absolutely no meaning.'

'That's all very well,' I mentioned, not going to be put down by smart-aleckery, 'that's all very well. But I happen to be living in the context of mortality.'

'If a man lives in a telephone box does that make him a button B? Alternatively, does it make the telephone box a house?'

'Well', I hedged, playing for time.

AND . . .

As luck would have it, at that moment Anna came out of the

house, carrying a basket full of wet clothes to hang on the line. Aoife hopped and skipped along beside her. It was a cosy domestic scene. Like an ad for wool carpets.

Anna winked at me as she passed. Her breasts bounced inside her T shirt. We were in love.

Life was GOOD.

'Who's that?' asked my resident voice.

'That's Anna, my wife.'

'I prefer slim girls', the voice replied. 'Something rather off-putting about women like that . . .'

'Well look here Mr Pearse . . . that's my wife and that's the sort of woman I like . . . we all know your problem. Mate.'

'I presume you are referring to my alleged latent homosexuality?'

'Precisely.'

Silence for a moment. Except for the humming of the motor mower, the chatter of little Aoife, the sound of birdsong, the buzzing of summer . . .

Peace, perfect peace . . . until . . .

Aoife, bored with watching her Mummy hanging up the washing, came and started hopping and skipping around the lawnmower.

'Don't do that, Aoife.'

'Why not?'

'Because you'll get your toes cut off, that's why.'

'What do I need toes for anyway?'

'You'd fall over if you had no toes.'

'No I wouldn't.'

'Yes you would.'

'No I wouldn't.'

'Yes you would. ANNA . . .'

'Yes Martin?'

'Would you mind removing this child from under the lawnmower?'

'Yes Martin. I would mind.'

'Oh come on for Christ's sake.'

'Don't say "Christ" in front of her.'

'Since when is Christ a dirty word?'

Anna, with her empty basket, approached. 'It's the inflexion you put on it, not the word itself.'

'Like string', I mentioned, leering at her chest.

She had the grace to blush. And then . . . ('Come with Mummy') . . . she grabbed Aoife's hand and off with the two of them to the back door.

I watched their backs. One looked like a scale model of the other. Aoife a small miniature Anna . . . . strange.

WHAT HAD HAPPENED TO MY GENES?

'They're hanging on the line', said the cynical voice of Patrick Pearse inside my head.

'Hah', I riposted quick as greased lightning, 'What do you know about jeans?'

'I keep up to date', he replied huffily.

I stopped the lawnmower. The grass was finished. A credit to the neighbourhood. (I don't believe that I've mentioned that I am the hon. sec. of the Residents' Association. Well I am.)

The grass was finished and now there was nothing to do but empty the grass box and put away the machine. AND ALSO . . . TO SORT OUT A FEW THINGS WITH MR PEARSE . . .

'Now look here Paddy,' I said, 'what's all this? What the hell are you doing inside my head? You're meant to be dead and safely buried up there in Arbour Hill with all your other mates.'

'No friends of mine, that lot', came the reply.

'How do you mean?'

'Never trusted any of them. Sure they would have had me up against a wall and shot me soon as look at me.'

'But the Brits got the lot of you first?'

'Precisely.'

Another small silence. As I walked to the compost heap with the grass cuttings. (Some horticulturists don't believe in putting grass cuttings on compost. But I do. And my garden is a living verification of my beliefs.)

'WELL?' I said, 'what are you doing in my head?'

'I'm in a manifestation.'

'Yes?'

'On an errand, so to speak.'

'An errand?'

'Yes. You see Deirdre of the Sorrows is in a manifestation too at the moment. I want to have a few words with her.'

'Where is she?'

'In Coolock. She's with a girl called Emily Farrell.'

'This is absurd.'

I sat down on the compost heap, for just a moment

wondering that if I sat there long enough would I rot down organically . . . return to Mother Earth . . . perhaps . . .

'This is absurd, fucking absurd. Why don't you talk to Deirdre of the Sorrows there . . . in heaven or wherever you lot are.'

'In The Beyond.'

'Well in The Beyond then. Why not talk to her there?'

There was an embarrassed silence. And then, in a small, humiliated voice, Paddy said 'it's not possible'.

'Why not?'

'We're in different sections.'

'Oh yes?'

He explained. The Beyond, apparently, is rigidly divided along tribal lines. And Patrick because of his ancestors, is in the English Section. Which, as one can appreciate, is absolutely intolerable for a man like him. Cut off from all his buddies, no-one but Oliver Cromwell, Ethelred The Unready and Winston Churchill to talk to. At least Eamon deValera, who is in the Spanish Section, at least he has Simon Bolivar and Che Guevara to hobnob with. Like-minded revolutionaries, so to speak. It appears that Eamon gets on particularly well with General Franco, the two of them, with Simon Bolivar and Che, forming a sort of pressure group within the overall set-up.

Not so Patrick Pearse.

He's totally alone. Cromwell bores him stiff. STIFF. And as for King Canute and guys like that . . . well . . . you might as well be talking to the wall . . .

'How then,' I asked, 'how did you hear about Deirdre of the Sorrows coming from Coolock?'

'I have informants. People keep me posted.'

'I see.'

I didn't, actually . . . but it seemed the right thing to say at the time.

6

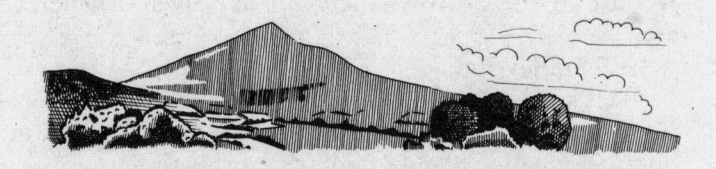

MOTHER-IN-LAW WAS STAYING to dinner. She had not quite recovered from her morning shock of discovering that her beloved daughter Anna had a penchant for being screwed on the kitchen table . . . but no matter.

Both Anna and I felt that, in the circumstances, the right and proper thing to do was to invite her to stay to dinner. To make it up to her, so to speak.

We all sat down around the table, all on our best behaviour, eating our spaghetti bolognese and making polite conversation.

AOIFE: This stuff is like worms, isn't it?
ANNA: No it's not.
SELF: Think of the starving black babies.
MOTHER-IN-LAW: Italians aren't black.

Mother-in-Law was a widow and I wasn't surprised. She'd drive any decent man to his grave. And, the old fella buried, she was now working on me. Harassing me. Trying to drive insidious little wedges between myself and Anna. Like:

1. When are you going to get a promotion in the ESB, Martin? I mean you're getting on a bit now. You don't want to be a clerk all your life, do you?

2. Anna I think you should get your hair cut. It's too long for a woman of your age.

3. When are you making your first Holy Communion, Aoife?

4. Anna I don't really think tight T-shirts suit you. I mean you are a bit big in that department. I mean a woman of your age . . .

Silently, I sat through this barrage of hassle, carefully sprinkling parmesan cheese over my bolognese at suitable intervals, quietly sipping my glass of Quinnsworth white wine. (We live with a certain amount of style, Anna and I.)

Patrick Pearse remained silent too, though he did at one stage say 'how do you put up with that old bag?', to which I did not reply. And so he left, in a huff, I suppose.

After the spaghetti we had applie pie. With cream. Mother-in-Law watched me dollop cream onto my plate. 'Shocking bad for you, Martin, a man of your age. Want to watch the cholesterol, you know.'

Anna laughed. 'Mother . . . he's only thirty-two.'

'Yes . . . but he's an OLD thirty-two, don't you think?'

Anna looked at me carefully.

Aoife looked at me carefully too, then turned to Anna. 'Does that mean Daddy'll be dead soon, Mummy?'

'Of course not, dear', replied the wife. Doubtfully.

I held my peace. Thoughtfully picked the £1.84 price tag off the wine bottle.

'Have you got life insurance, Martin?' asked Mother-in-Law.

'Not a penny', I lied. 'Après moi, la deluge. Anna and Aoife will starve. Shocking. It'll be the streets for Anna, the orphanage for Aoife.' I shook my head sadly.

'Of course he has life insurance, mother', said Anna. 'Don't mind him.' She looked at me menacingly, a look that implied that the next game with string in the bedroom would be called STRANGULATION – A GAME FOR ALL THE FAMILY.

I smiled sweetly.

Things went from bad to worse.

And, when she had satisfied herself that our marriage was on the rocks, Mother-in-Law went home. She was worried about her cat, a poor emasculated tom that was serving a life sentence in her house and had made several escape attempts already.

* * *

'But I WASN'T rude to her', I protested as I took off my underpants prior to getting into bed, not the best time to make a really effective protest perhaps . . . but there we are . . .

'Yes you WERE', insisted Anna, sitting up in that same bed madly wrapping string around one of her lampshades. Her nerves were at her. I could tell the state of her nerves by the speed at which she manufactured lampshades. 'Yes you WERE.'

'She's an old bat anyway', I suggested, moodily looking down at my dangling manhood and consoling myself with the thought that it was only from this angle that it looked so unimpressive. Or so I hoped.

'She's my MOTHER.'

I leaped into the bed. It was a mistake. My bare bottom landed onto one of Anna's lampshade making implements, a device which, on removing it from my anus, I decided looked like a yoke for castrating bulls. 'Holy Shit', I said, 'will you be careful with your damn tools.'

'You likewise', muttered Anna, her nimble fingers whirring madly about the wirework on the half made shade. In and out, in and out . . .

I watched. Until my patience was exhausted. Not an overly extended length of time. 'How long,' I ventured, 'how long are you going to be engaged upon that foolish activity?'

'As long as it takes.'

'Well I'm feeling . . . a little . . . you know . . .'

'Take your hand off my leg.'

'Yes Anna. Sorry Anna.'

Her fingers whirred on. And there was silence. Until she said, 'and kindly remove your slavering lips from my tit. I'm not in the mood.'

'Yes Anna, sorry Anna.'

'And stop SAYING that.'

'Yes Anna, sorry Anna.'

'Go to sleep.'

'I don't want to go to sleep. As a matter of fact I want to tie you to the bed and whip you with your suspender belt.'

Anna giggled, her fingers paused. 'Do you?'

'Yes', I replied, replacing my hand on her thigh and my slavering lips to her breast. 'Yes I really do.'

Anna giggled again. 'Since when have you had these unnatural urges?'

'Oh for ages . . . ages and ages . . .' With immense subtlety I moved my hand up her thigh, testing it for firmness and texture with little strokes and squeezes en route, eventually arriving at her pubic hair which, with further immense subtlety, I combed with my fingertips.

'You're a crude bugger, aren't you', said Anna . . . 'TELL ME . . .' She threw her lampshade gear onto the floor . . . 'Tell me do you ever think of anything but sex?'

'Not when I'm in bed with you', I replied, astonishing myself with this charm.

Anna sat back, put her hands behind her head, looked at me quietly. And I looked at her, equally quietly, deciding that, handled rightly, this could be a BEAUTIFUL MOMENT. And I am very fond of beautiful moments. At heart, I am a poet. Whereas, at heart, Anna is a sex-mad fiend.

Poetry and lust make great bedfellows.

Anna looked at me quietly, her face serene, the little flickers of her tongue across her lips the only hint to that sex-mad fiendish personality of hers.

I looked at her quietly.

The contrast between her pretty-little-girl face framed with trickles of blonde hair . . . the contrast between her face and her body attracted me strongly.

Because . . . well . . . let me put it this way . . . Anna is a hefty bird. There's a lot of her. She wallows, rather than lies, in a bed. And to-night the massive billows of her breasts brought to mind an image of two bloated octupuses hanging on for dear life.

Octupii?

No matter. With a great ROAR I leapt up on her . . .

7

PATRICK PEARSE AND I woke up together. It was scarcely dawn. The shadows of the dark hours drifted by my eyes. I saw a grey light outside the window. The house still, smelling of night.

'WELL', said Patrick Pearse, a revolting HEALTHY tone to his voice, 'Well let's get to it, old chap. No sense in hanging around here. Time and tide await no man and all that sort of thing.'

'I'm tired', I replied, 'for Jesus sake ... it's the middle of the bloody night.' I curled up and buried my face in Anna's octupuses. I mean breasts. But the images of the night before, like dreams not faded yet, the images were still alive in my mind.

'TIRED?' said Patrick, 'tired? Well is it any wonder, all that carry-on here last night. Damn it man ... sex is draining your life blood. Did you never think of celibacy?'

'No', I replied, Anna's left octopus enfolding my face with a soft white whomph. 'No, I never considered celibacy. So piss off and leave me alone.'

'Out of the question. I've only got to-day. After that you can do what you like, for all I care. Though mark my words, you can only go downhill ... oh yes ... those slippery slopes of lust ... oh yes ...'

He went on and on. For some time I endured the sanctimonious waffle, trying to close out his words, using Anna's flesh as earplugs. So to speak. But, because his voice was inside my head, there was no stopping him.

TO HELL WITH IT.

Anna muttered sleepy mutters. Her hot little hands were clamped about my upper leg. I would not have been averse to sliding slightly further down the slippery slopes of lust ... but

. . . to hell with it . . .

It was impossible.

Gently, I disengaged myself from my better half, got up, stood stupidly naked in the centre of the room.

'Well get some clothes on man . . . I suggest something in the line of a harris tweed jacket, cavalry twills, perhaps a cravat.'

'What are you talking about? I haven't got clothes like that.'

'Mmmm', said Patrick, thoughtfully. 'Well that's a pity. I mean to say . . . we ARE going to see Deirdre of the Sorrows. It'd be nice to be dressed suitably.'

'Well,' I mentioned mockingly, 'I could wear my father's old Volunteer uniform, slouch hat and all that bit.'

'That's an idea,' he replied eagerly, 'get it on and let me see how you look.'

It was terrible to disappoint the man. But I had to explain that my father, far from being in the Volunteers, had been in Trinity College Dublin at the time of Patrick's revolution. In fact, so family history rumoured, old dad had led a horde of egg-throwing undergrads to hassle the revolutionaries on their way to the prison camps.

Our family fortunes had gone downhill ever since.

But be that as it may. Patrick made a few grumpy remarks about the decadent ascendancy and suchlike of that ilk; I dressed in my normal on-leave-from-ESB gear of blue jeans, hush-puppy bootees, lumberjack shirt.

'Good grief', said Patrick Pearse.

'Where are you off to', asked Anna, waking up and looking rarely beautiful, tousled and desirable.

'Well', I murmured . . .

'Well?' she inquired, tilting her head to one side, absent-mindedly running her right index finger in concentric circles around her left nipple.

'Well', I said again. 'WELL.'

It hardly seemed appropriate to say that I was going off to see Deirdre of the Sorrows in Coolock. No. Anna was a tolerant and understanding girl. BUT . . . perhaps now is the time to mention that before I married her she was a psychiatric nurse in John of God's . . . this being so she was always on the alert for mental disorder in her friends, acquaintances, husband too.

Old habits die hard.

So. I decided to lie.

'I'm going on a picnic.'

'A PICNIC??? At seven o'clock in the morning?' Anna raised herself up on her elbows, staring at me with that psychiatric nurse's expression which I knew so well. Defiantly, I stared back, noticing in the meantime how her white breasts had surfaced from under the blue sheets, like whales coming up to play in the blue and desolate waters of some far away and southern sea.

'A PICNIC?', she repeated, 'have you fallen out of your tree? Get back into bed THIS INSTANT you silly man you.'

Well. I admit. A picnic did sound ridiculous. So I changed my story. Immediately and brilliantly. With all the flair of a politician in a tight corner.

'I'm going fishing with Walter.'

'Fishing? You don't fish.'

'Well I thought I'd give it a try. Feel it might relax me. I have these tensions.'

Yes. Nice one that. Almost believed it myself, could see the quiet riverbank scene in my mind . . . sunlight trickling down through trees, water wriggling along by mossy stones . . . yes . . . and me with a little hat, a fish hook stuck in it, my cheese sandwiches and bottle of stout in my army surplus webbing bag beside me on the grass. Could see it all. And the day that was in it. Right down to the German anglers further up the river, equipped like a Panzer division, coldly and efficiently massacreing celtic fish, their pale blue eyes gazing at the water.

Yes. I could see it all. Felt it might relax me.

'Come back into bed and I'll relax you', Anna murmured, lasciviously stretching her fat little arms above her head, arching her stomach and pubic regions upwards.

'That woman's on heat', muttered Patrick Pearse.

'Shut up', I replied. To him. To Anna I explained that Walter was waiting for me down at his house and there was no time to be lost and I'd see her at tea time if not before and anyway wasn't she going to-day to a hen party in Dundrum for mums and kids and what did she need me hanging about for?

Sure I'd only be in the way.

And after all . . . let's face it . . . life must have these little partings. Or how could we ever say hello . . .?

'Suit yourself', she said, rolling over onto her tummy, thereby exposing to my wistful eye the length of one leg and the big white massiveness of half her bottom. And the agreeable oozing out from under her of the flesh of one fat white breast, the whiteness of this even whiter than the whiteness of the rest of her. As if she washed her breasts in Daz, other parts of her body merely in some cheap Brand X.

Knowing I was looking at her, no doubt sensing my lust . . . (women have their instincts . . . it's their glands) . . . knowing I was looking at her, Anna wriggled her shoulders a fraction, a little muscular contraction running down her back, elevating her bottom by a small amount, perhaps three quarters of an inch or its metric equivalent . . . a small amount . . . but enough.

'Definitely,' said Patrick Pearse, 'on heat. Can't the medical profession do anything for her? We had cats in father's stone yard, behaved like that. Remember them well. Used to send for the vet.'

'My wife is not a cat', I replied shortly, the meantime resting my right hand in a proprietorial fashion on the girl in question's thigh.

'No offence, old chap. But females ARE females.'

'A lot you'd know about that.' My proprietorial hand moved up Anna's thigh, following the awesome curves of her buttocks admiringly.

'Alright alright', said Patrick Pearse. 'Touché touché. Now can we please be on our way? Or are you going to spend the whole day fondling the woman's backside?'

'OK OK', I said. He was right. It was time to go. I kissed Anna on the back of the head, carefully draped the blankets over her exposed areas, and departed. Out the bedroom door and down the stairs. Down the eighteen steps of my stairs . . . of which, I had once calculated, I was the owner of one point seven three six threads . . .

The Building Society owned the rest.

8

NATURALLY, LIKE THE next man, I am very interested in The Beyond and just what exactly is going on there. And, having Patrick Pearse with me as I drove into the city that morning, well, it was too good an opportunity to be missed. So I asked him certain questions. Not that the answers given were very satisfactory. Paddy, if the truth were known, is very bored with The Beyond and far more interested in looking out the window, seeing the changes that time has wrought to the city.

However, though with some difficulty, I did manage to get him to tell me a little about The Beyond. Not that I wasn't interested in his opinions on Modern Ireland, no, but opinions on Modern Ireland are two a penny really. The air in pubs is thick with them . . . magazines, newspapers, novels, church newsletters . . . polluted with opinions, opinions of opinions, not to mention opinions of opinions of opinions. The Common Man, that Man on The Clapham Omnibus, much loved of English Journalists, is everywhere in Ireland. It sometimes seems that, since the days of the horse tram, all the Clapham omnibuses have disgorged their loads of opinionated ignorati on the doorsteps of Dublin pubs, on the steps of Government offices, in the marble and mahogany halls where editors postulate, in the bedsitters of struggling young writers who, though their talent be likened to the male nipple in the intrinsic wonder of its uselessness, will have their books and pamphlets published by socialist co-operative as a gesture of solidarity with their fellow illiterates and THEREBY . . . add THEIR opinions to the great pyramid of opinions which, balancing hugely and precariously over our little island, threatens daily to force us down beneath the waves thus fulfilling that prophecy that Ireland would be drowned rather than consumed by fire . . .

So. Cognisant of all this, I mercilessly pumped Patrick for news of The Beyond. At my age, in my delicate state of health, as I prepare to join that great and noble procession of O'Sheas who have gone to their just reward, The Beyond is of immediate concern. And what I learned from Patrick Pearse is this . . .

Firstly, it appears, The Beyond is not really The Beyond at all. To explain . . . one will remember learning at school that for God there was no Past, no Present, no Future . . . well . . . that's the way it is.

The Beyond IS. And that's that.

We don't go THERE from HERE. As soon as we're HERE, we're also THERE. So to speak. As soon as we're conceived, we're already in The Beyond. The fact that some are alive and kicking while others are stiff and dead . . . well that has nothing to do with it.

Life and Death is a continuum.

'What do people DO in The Beyond, Patrick?' I asked him while temporarily held up at the level crossing on the Merrion Road.

'Well,' he replied thoughtfully, 'it's not that they DO anything, really. Well you see . . . it's difficult to explain . . . but people aren't really PEOPLE in The Beyond.'

'Could you perhaps be more explicit?'

'No.'

'I see.'

We waited in silence. And then a train thundered past, huge and mighty and magnificent. Patrick looked at it thoughtfully.

'They don't use steam anymore?'

'No. Diesel electric. Though there's going to be electrification on all the suburban lines. From Bray to Skerries.'

'A good idea, in my opinion. Man should make the best use of all available technology.'

The gates swung open. I drove over. And proceeded along towards Sandymount. It was eight o'clock, or thereabouts. Early commuters trundled along in front and behind. A man walked a dog. A man and woman jogged by together in matching tracksuits. One was sure they were in advertising and had stripped the floorboards in their living room down to the bare wood and given them a coat or two of polyurethane.

Certain things, one knows.

'Look at those chimneys', Patrick chortled.

I looked, across the bay to the twin ESB erections. I had seen them before. In fact there was a photograph of them in Head Office which I could look at daily if I so wished.

'Just look at those chimneys', Patrick chortled again. 'Isn't that's a wonderful sight to see?'

'Sure is', I murmured.

'So symbolic of the new Ireland arising from the ashes of the old . . . towering monuments reaching for the sky . . . grasping, as it were, grasping out for the things of heaven, the spiritual values so sorely needed in a mundane world.'

He paused for breath. I took the opportunity to get my oar in.

'Well actually they're merely there so folks can have electricity, for their colour tellys on which to watch Coronation Street, for their deep freezes, electric razors and many other household appliances too numerous to mention. That's what those chimneys are for. Really.'

'HAH', riposted Patrick, 'there are many ways of looking at the world, Martin O'Shea, if you choose to wallow in the gutter of materialism and base carnal greed then that's your prerogative. All the children of the nation shall be cherished equally. Even the creeps like you.'

'Glad to hear it', I mentioned.

* * *

We were now in Ringsend. Streets of little houses, large juggernauts, old ladies, bookies shops and girls in serge dresses.

Over the bridge with us.

Past the great hulk of the dogtrack stands. Past gasworks and bus stations and scrap yards and motorbike factories and surgical bed factories and small corner newsagents selling the Daily Mirror. And a dead dog with red innards by the side of the road. Two children poking at it with a stick. This vision somehow redolent of my spaghetti bolognese of the night before.

'Aahhh', said Patrick Pearse, 'the old place hasn't changed much . . .'

'Haven't you been,' I asked by way of conversation, 'haven't you been here since nineteen-sixteen?'

'Course I have. I was here in sixty-six, for the celebrations.' He paused moodily. 'Wasn't a successful manifestation though.'

'Why was that?'

'Oh . . . someone made a bags of it.' He sighed heavily. 'The Beyond, you know, is just as bogged down in bureaucracy as this place here. There I was, waiting fifty years for my manifestation application to come through . . . fifty long years . . . and what do you know . . .

'What do I know?'

'Well when it does come through I find myself with a failed clerical student living with a discharged nun in a double bed-sitter on the Harolds Cross Road.'

'That was hard luck', I agreed.

'Terrible. They had a gas ring to cook on and problems in the extra-marital bed. As a matter of fact they had problems with the gas ring too. There you'd be, boiling up a packet of Cuppasoup, boiling merrily away on the Woolworth's saucepan . . . when . . whoop . . . the gas would go off.'

'For no reason?'

'None at all. We lived on luke-warm Cuppasoup, damp erections and the Daily Telegraph.'

'You mean you ATE the Daily Telegraph? ' I asked him in amazement.

'Don't be absurd. We read it. The discharged nun was on the extreme right. Politically.'

'The two of you must have got on well then?'

'Well we did and we didn't. She was a bit EXTREME for me. She thought the blacks should be sterilised.'

'What blacks?'

'All the blacks where she'd spent ten years on the missions. It seems she'd given the best years of her life to them. Teaching them to read and write, distributing second-hand copies of religious magazines sent by pious people from the rural parishes of Ireland . . . ten long years . . . sweating it out . . . her young womanhood draining away like the juice of an orange into the dry tropical sky . . . ten long years . . . and THEN . . .'

'Then what?' I asked, carefully guiding the car into Tara Street, a difficult corner that . . . my paintwork was precious to me.

'Then there was a coup. Law and Order broke down. The mission was sacked by rampaging gangs of mutinous soldiers. The students rose up against the nuns too.'

'That's what comes of being brought up on secondhand copies of religious magazines', I amusingly interjected.

'No need to be irreligious.'

'Sorry.'

'Alright. WELL . . . I was saying . . . the mission was sacked. The nuns were all raped and generally brutalised, being kept locked up in a hut naked and hungry while the soldiers and students were raping and generally brutalising elsewhere.'

'Then what happened?'

'European parachutists arrived out of the sky like avenging angels.'

'What did they do?'

'Killed everyone.'

'Oh.'

A thoughtful silence from both Patrick Pearse and me. As we crossed Butt Bridge. We both reflected on the intricacies of international politics.

'Of course they didn't kill the nuns. They gave them blankets and food and were generally very kind. I suppose the nuns reminded them of their sisters. Back home in Bruges or somewhere.'

'That's life. Family ties are perhaps the strongest forces in human society . . .'

'Yes, yes. Of course the parachutists weren't so kind to all the black girls they could find. They raped them and committed unpleasant atrocities like cutting off their breasts with bayonets.'

'Oh', I said, shocked, and a small moment of silence descended as I pondered, not for the first time, the horrors of the Dark Continent. I made a mental note to cut back drastically my monthly donations to Oxfam, Concern, Help the Aged, Feed the People and The Itinerants Resettlement Committee. And to cancel my subscriptions to An Phoblacht, Magill, The Listener, The Economist and Newsweek. In this savage world, it struck me, the wise man should keep his head down, his decks clear, his powder dry and his own counsel . . .

Patrick Pearse broke the little silence . . .

'So . . . to cut a long story short . . . this nun, the girl friend to be of the failed clerical student in the Harold's Cross Road, she arrived back in Dublin wearing a Belgian army combat jacket, a pair of blue jeans and carrying a FN automatic rifle in a holdall.'

'What happened?'

'The special branch confiscated the rifle. Even though she said it was only for protection against rapacious blacks.'

'What did the Special Branch say?'

'Well they said there was no blacks in Dublin, rapacious or otherwise, and as far as they were concerned that was the way it was going to stay. AND FURTHERMORE, there were no ex-nuns with automatic rifles either . . . and as far as they were concerned . . .'

'That was the way it was going to stay?' I interrupted.

'Precisely.'

'Very conservative, the Special Branch . . .'

'Always were. Even back in my day . . . hey . . . where are you going, this isn't the way to Coolock . . .'

'Well I thought I'd hop up to Bewley's for a cup of coffee and a couple of cherry buns. If YOU REMEMBER . . . I missed my breakfast. On account of you.'

Patrick Pearse looked at my watch. He agreed, reluctantly, that early as it was, we would have time to go to Bewleys. Deirdre of the Sorrows out in Coolock probably wasn't even up yet.

I parked the car in Anne Street. Which always reminds me of my wife. Every time I walked along Anne Street I think of her breasts. Strange old world, the kingdom of the mind. Or perhaps I should say, with deference to Mr Pearse . . . the republic of the mind. But what the hell. I parked the car.

9

BEWLEY'S IS A rum old place. Thin-legged waitresses weave among mahogany tables. Early morning sun dances down through stained glass windows. Chaps read The Irish Times. The waitresses have thin lips too. They know their places. They know their regular customers' faces.

But not mine.

'A large white coffee. And a couple of cherry buns, please.'

'Right you be.'

I watch her skeletal bottom walk away. And think of death.

'So, Patrick, so what happened then?'

'What happened when?' asked Patrick, looking vaguely about.

'Strange place this, eh? Why aren't all these people at work?'

'For God's sake,' I said, looking at my watch, 'it's only just after nine...'

'Hah... they're at work in Frankfurt, Brussels or New York right now... in fact they've done a half day's work by now. My word you're a lazy bunch... is it any wonder...'

'Stop being so British, Patrick.'

'Sorry. It's in my blood.'

'Ok. Tell me about the ex-nun, she fascinates me.'

'Well', he said, starting to speak and then pausing while the waitress returned with my coffee, my side plate, my knife, my little saucer of foil-wrapped butter pats, my plate of buns miscellaneous.

'Well,' he continued, when she had departed, 'well the poor woman arrived in Busarus from the airport with only the clothes she stood up in and the rest of her ticket back to the Mother House of her order in rural Monaghan. To which place she did not wish to go. However, as luck would have it she fell into conversation with a young typist from the Department of Lands who it just so happened was about to buy a ticket to

Monaghan for the purpose of going home for the weekend to see her boyfriend and go dancing. Big Tom and the Mainliners were playing in the GAA hall that weekend.'

'You've a great memory for detail.'

'It's the trained mind. Can't beat the trained mind, Martin.'

'You're right there.'

'Sure I am. Don't forget I was a schoolteacher for many years in St Enda's.'

'Whatever happened to St Enda's?'

'I have no idea.'

'Aren't you interested?'

'Not particularly. A man grows out of things. Now do you want to hear the rest of the story or not?'

'Carry on', I waved my coffee cup at him. 'Carry on.'

'So the ex-nun, what did she do? She sold her ticket at cut price to this young one. And they were both happy. The ex-nun had a few pounds in her pocket, the young one had saved the price of four vodkas and coke . . . everyone was happy.'

'Delighted for them.'

'Mmmm. Anyhow, out of Busarus goes the ex-nun, still in her Belgian army combat jacket and blue jeans. Out she goes. Up along the quays towards Phoenix Park.'

'Why was she going there?'

'I have no idea. In any case she never reached it.'

'Oh?'

'No. You see at the Ha'penny Bridge a man lept out of the shadows and said "givus sixpence for a cuppa tea, missus".'

'Don't tell me . . . it was the failed clerical student?'

'Right. Your man himself. Fallen on hard times. It's a harsh old world for a failed clerical student. It was the dogmatic theology that got him in the end.'

'Gets a lot of people, dogmatic theology.'

'Yes. Anyhow. The two of them fell into conversation and gradually realised that they had a lot in common, two waifs in an uncaring world, that sort of thing. In no time at all they had set themselves up in the Harolds Cross bedsitter, she working making sandwiches in Graham O'Sullivan's and he writing the definitive Irish novel which had been commissioned from him by The O'Brien Press, a Distinguished Publishing House.'

'An interesting little household.'

'Absolutely. Marred only by their difficulties in the sexual arena. You see they both had problems.'

'I'm not surprised.'

'Yes. Every time he attempted to approach her in bed she, imagining she was back in Africa, would scream and try to strangle him.'

'The neighbours must have loved that carry-on.'

'Yes. Anyhow, one evening she came home from work and there was your man, stark naked, covered in black shoe polish. Out he leaps, throws her to the floor, rips the flimsy fabric off and has his way with her. And, here's the strange thing, not a peep out of her. She gave as good as she got.'

'The human mind is a strange old thing.'

'Nothing stranger. Anyway. That was the solution. From then on he would black up every night.'

'Must've been expensive in shoe polish.'

'Well it was for a while. But then he bought some of that theatrical make-up that people use when doing Al Jolson impersonations . . . found that more economical. Easier to wash off in the morning when he had to go out to Rathmines Library to do research for his definitive Irish novel . . .'

I sipped my coffee thoughtfully. 'Do you,' I said, 'do you expect me to believe A WORD of this absurd anecdote?'

Patrick Pearse laughed.

And as he laughed I suddenly realised one explanation for the man's extraordinary life, extraordinary death . . . deep down, far below the depths of dreams and anger, deep down he had a place where a little boy laughed, a place where things were strange but simple, quiet but full of merry goings-on . . .

Deep down he was an innocent.

An Íosagán.

A magnificent man.

10

A MAGNIFICENT MAN, I thought. How nice to be sitting here in Bewley's in the company of such a chap, my dead leader . . . or maybe, like Dracula, my undead leader, forever with me, the prophet of my country, conscience of my people . . . keeper of the keys.

How nice . . . but strange . . . though maybe apt . . . yes definitely apt that the undead leader should be some class of an Englishman. Yes yes yes . . . . nice and suitable and APT in this age of reconciliation between nations, war thankfully a thing of the benighted past . . . how apt that my country cleaves to its somewhat wrinkled bosom an image of itself as perpetrated by foreign celtiphobes much in the manner of a modern Scot wearing a kilt and tossing telephone poles around Edinburgh in memory of Queen Victoria who when all is said and done invented modern Scotland because she loved Balmoral and probably John Brown too. God Bless the old lady. Those were the days. The pound was worth a pound. And the sun never set . . .

How nice to be sitting here in Bewley's with a panache owing little to economics when one could and probably should be at one's desk in the ESB, busy doing a decent day's work writing letters to cranks not to mention looking out the window to keep an eye on the unemployed out there plotting in pub doorways while they wait for opening time. Must be watched, that lot. For two pins or more likely two pints they'd remember Connolly another foreigner come to think of it sticking his socialist nose into our affairs . . . for two pints the unemployed would vote for a Workers' Republic and next minute it's the bloody Lebanon or Iran and up against the wall at dawn with Martin O'Shea an enemy of the people. Too damn right. They must be watched.

Well. Yes, one COULD be at one's desk. An interesting old piece of furniture just by-the-by which I'd inherited from generations of dead Clerical Officers, its surface gouged with initials, ink stains, faded doodles and the telephone numbers of long dead girlfriends of the twenties . . . where are they now . . . long dead long legged girls of long ago . . . silky thighs . . . dangling beads over small pointed breasts . . . and wind-up gramophones in the suburbs of Rathgar, red-bricked once and leafy-laned, faded now and drab though trendy, haunt of Malaysian medical students, bald homosexuals in basement flats, media men, publishers . . . and accounts executives from the lesser advertising agencies. Sad sad sad.

Sad but interesting. One's old desk, one's crutch passed down through crippled generations. Interesting . . . one got a sense of continuity, sitting there, a link with the past. One was one with the weary procession of day-to-day man on his journey to the grave.

'How long have you been in the ESB, Martin?', asked Patrick Pearse, as if reading my thoughts . . .

'Oh . . . long enough . . . long enough . . .' I sipped my coffee.

'Would you classify it as a career . . . in the ESB? I mean to say . . . has it any future?'

'Oh indubitably . . .' I smiled, that wan, half-defeated smile that I normally reserved for seducing a certain type of caring-in-an-ongoing-context woman. 'Sure it has a future. One day I'll end up like Myles Flannery.'

'Who on earth is Myles Flannery?' Patrick was perplexed.

'He's not on earth. He's dead. In The Beyond. With you lot. Haven't you met him there?'

'Can't say I have,' Patrick mused, 'though there is a Flann or some such, over in section BX 12 C . . . gloomy sort of chap . . . fond of a drink I feel . . .'

'Probably Flann O'Brien', I realised, remembering the writer who had amused me in my youth . . . before I understood what he was on about . . . before I noticed how the words rattled, desperate dry dead bones on the page . . . 'Yes. Probably Flann O'Brien . . . different man entirely . . . what's section BX 12 C anyway?'

'Well its the overflow from section BX 12 B. And THAT'S the overflow from BX 12 A. All the BX 12 sections are reserved for writers who drank themselves to death. Packed out, those sections . . . lot of agitation going on for better conditions . . . impossible situation really . . . as soon as the powers that be improve things, open a new overflow, along come a new crowd, squatting down like tinkers, demanding rights and privileges and grants-in-aid from the Happy Committee . . .'

'The WHHAA???'

'The Happy Committee.' Patrick looked embarrassed. As well he might. 'It's a sort of . . . well . . . how shall I put it . . . much like the Arts Council here on earth . . . supports deprived sections of the Beyond community . . .'

'So, Patrick, what have you got against tinkers anyway?'

'I didn't do anything AGAINST them . . . merely said that chaps came into The Beyond . . . and squatted down . . . like tinkers . . .'

'An implication there, I feel. You implied that they're a dirty bunch of antisocial knackers who'd live in your ear and take the eye out of your head if you blinked.'

'Nothing of the sort. In my view tinkers embody some of the traditional Irish qualities. Recent sociological observations on the sub-culture have reinforced my opinions.'

'True, true', I agreed, seeing in that mind's eye which is the bliss of Bewley's a tinker encampment full of bare-footed brats, squalor, empty Guinness bottles and American journalists doing research to fill in the gaps in their notebooks between Cambodia, the sex lives of oil sheikhs, worker-priests in Bolivia and the latest Breakthrough in Cancer.

'HAH', I spluttered into my cup, my xenophobic hatred of foreigners with typewriters boiling over and reheating the coffee in a pleasantly energy-saving way. 'Hah. Tinkers. Sociologists. Slums. More sociologists. Every shit heap in the world attracts the swine like flies, buzzing along from atrocity to horror, from man's inhumanity to man to the last of the pink panthers . . . buzz buzz buzz . . . then back home to their campus apartments with the Bang and Olufsen quadrophonic and the poster of Jane Fonda withering picturesquely under her menopause on the wall. Hah.'

When I am Taoiseach, I decided, all tinkers shall be given one bath and sent to Connaught. All typewriters, recorders, notebooks shall be confiscated from foreigners at points of entry to the NATION.

'Hah', I said, one more time, and then I swallowed. 'Sure they know no better. It's society's fault that has them the way they are.'

'Who?'

'Tinkers. And these bloody foreign writers . . . ten minutes in Dublin Airport carpark and they know it all. Bloody Miracle. Jesus. The O'Sheas have been in this country for ten thousand years and we still haven't a clue about what's going on.'

'Sometimes the outside observer . . .' mused Paddy. And then, with more emphasis, 'well I hope you don't include ME in the category of "bloody foreign writers"?'

I smiled. And the mystic mirror on the wall, the wall of that little room where I keep my past all safe and neat like a Sunday suit in a cupboard, the mirror smiled right back at me. My smile, my lips, my eyes inherited from long dead peasants on tatty mountainsides, gloomy men, dark people with lumps of rocks in their hands, cudgels in their fists, gloomy men, mad with rage and fear of Gods and hate of other tribes. Smiling all the time. My smile. Everywhere. Irish eyes are smiling. And old Gods darkly wait behind our eyes.

'Take that smirk off your face', said Patrick Pearse.

'That smirk is my inscrutable smile . . . I'm practising for the Chinese restaurant I'm thinking of opening. Pale Moon of The Single Sadness, that's what I'll call it.' The idea took hold. I waved my arms about excitedly. Folks at nearby tables vanished into their newspapers. Lest their own madnesses bubble to the surface. 'Yes. Pale Moon of The Single Sadness . . . birds in oriental gear . . . skirts slashed to the hip . . . water chestnuts . . . bamboo shoots . . . fried rice fifteen pence extra . . . what d' you think?'

'Sometimes I think . . . sometimes I have grave doubts . . .' he began.

'About your sanity', I completed the sentence for him. 'So you want to hear about Myles Flannery of the ESB?'

'Myles Flannery is irrelevant', said Patrick, in the testy manner of a priest in the confession box realising that he is about to hear from some young one about how her fella sucked her nipple and she went all gooey in her tummy and couldn't help it and said yes oh yes I said yes and yes oh yes oh Jesus. Rhododendrons. Howth. James Joyce. Ah well. Went mad in the end. Blind as a bat. Daft as a brush. Ah well . . . died in

Zurich. Buried with the gnomes.

'Myles Flannery? Irrelevant?' I was shocked. 'NO MAN IS IRRELEVANT', I announced grandiosely. 'We all have our parts to play. All the world's a stage. And all the men and women merely players. William Shakespeare.'

'I know. I know I know', said Patrick Pearse tiredly.

'Ah yes . . .' I pointed meaningfully, 'but did you know that he was an Irishman?'

Patrick Pearse looked at me coldly.

* * *

My first boss in the ESB was a man called Myles Flannery. He was of the old school, Myles, lived alone in digs somewhere off the South Circular Road and cycled to work on a black Rudge with a complete chain guard. You don't see many of them these days.

Myles was a crusty old bachelor, I suppose . . . but a decent sort. He didn't ask much from life, didn't get much either. A solitary pint in the evening . . . maybe . . . a lonely masturbation in his furnished room . . . perhaps . . .

Whether he ever loved or danced or even laughed I do not know. Certainly I never saw him laugh. And whether he ever loved . . . or danced . . . well . . . that I have no way of knowing.

The only thing that I do know about Myles is that he loved his bicycle, the shiny black Rudge with the green piping, the high and shiny old-fashioned handlebars, the complete chain guard.

He loved that bicycle.

And, as sometimes happens, the thing he loved was his downfall.

It happened like this. Every morning he'd come in to work, chain the bike to the railings outside Head Office. This was in the old days when Head Office was a magnificent Georgian structure, shortly before the new erection as designed by some up and coming architect whose name I have forgotten already, thus anticipating the verdict of history.

So. Old Myles chained his Rudge to the railings every

morning. And then one day, one terrible day, when they were starting to demolish the old buildings by removing the railings ... well ... it's easy to guess ... the ignorant slobs of demolition workers just shagged poor old Myles's bike into the lorry and off with the lot to the Hammond Lane foundry to be melted down for the manufacture of surgical beds or back boilers what you can heat six radiators off if you can afford coal. So. Out from work that evening comes Myles, his bicycle clips on his ankles where else ... looks about at the dereliction ... realises what's happened ... has a coronary thrombosis and drops down dead as an election manifesto on the pavement. Dead.

Typists screamed, rushing about like hens, then rushing home to tell their bedsitter mates about it. Then, no doubt, rushing off to discos to buy expensive glasses of cheap wine ... to meet married men from Dundrum with whom to perform sex acts in the backs of company owned Cortinas. Sex acts which, it must be added lest slander be cast on the moral virtues of female ESB clerical workers, sex acts which must NOT involve carnal penetration 'cos that's going TOO far and the girls are saving their ultimates for lads with a decent farm of land in Roscommon ... saving their money to build bungalows with labour saving devices particularly ceramic wipe-clean hobs and eye-level ovens as advertised in Woman's Way between the articles about fashion designer Pat Crowley and wife-of-ex-Taoiseach, Maureen Lynch.

And what it's like to be married.

To The Man.

Yes. Typists. Sex acts. Married men from Dundrum. Even a Married Man From Glenageary must confess to having succumbed once or twice to the blandishments of girls with strange exotic rural accents, allowing himself to be enticed away from his much-loved wife, finding himself indulging in culchie perversions, the three most notable of which are

The Ankle in the Ashtray

The Penis Between the Breasts

And The Gear Lever In the Small of The Back.

However. The typists screamed when old Myles died. Hither and thither they rushed. And he lay dead on the pavement. Ambulances, priests and police were called ... but could do nothing ... except carry out their official functions. And the next day the lads in the section drew lots to see who'd go to the funeral up in Glasnevin and I won. Or lost, I'm not sure which. I went anyway.

And it rained.

* * *

'It usually does,' said Patrick Pearse 'No funeral seems to be complete without a drop of rain.'

'Part of the action,' I agreed, 'a funeral without rain is like an office Christmas party without a feel up behind the filing cabinets and someone vomiting into a waste paper basket.'

'In the ESB?' Patrick was horrified.

'You better believe it. Sodom and Gomorrah isn't in it on Christmas Eve. The year before last Monica from Claremorris dressed up in twenty-six feet of computer printout paper with details of debtors recalcitrant on it. Did a sort of dance of the seven veils on a desk top.'

'What happened?'

'She unravelled.'

'Good grief.'

'Don't panic. Six months later she was married to a farmer in Kiltimagh and now she's a mother and a member of the Irish Countrywomen's Association where she won a prize for best sponge cake at a bring 'n' buy sale in aid of Gorta . . . fell on her feet that girl . . .'

'Glad to hear it.'

'Yes. Though have you noticed how most women who spend their younger years falling on their backs for all and sundry suddenly up and fall on their feet . . . have you noticed that?'

'Can't say I have. Of course I don't have your experience of the seamier side of life.'

'Jesus you sanctimonious prick. What about slaughtering all those poor English soldiers in 1916 . . . not to mention the innocent citizens who'd be sitting in their beds of a quiet bank holiday maybe having a quick shunt with the missus and next minute a republican shell comes through the ceiling and splatt . . . what about that for the seamier side of life?'

'War is hell. Anyway they were British shells . . . we only had light weapons.'

'Just as bloody well if you ask me.'

'Our strength was the rightness of our cause.'

* * *

At Myles Flannery's funeral there was only me and two gravediggers and a priest who looked tired and two small brown birds searching for brown worms in the brown clay and it broke my heart. I stood there looking about me at the graves of my ancestors, proud and humble both . . . stood in the rain thinking about life and death but mostly death and mostly not the death of great men who had fine marble tombs with fine words on them . . . no . . . the lives and the deaths of the proud and famous were obscured and forgotten by the fine noble memories.

Humble people live longer.

Shivering in the rain among the graves, I could see their shadows still, the folks who'd played bit parts. And one was a pretty girl in a tram window in Dorset Street in nineteen hundred and eight. And another was a man who saw her face in the window passing. And he smiled at her and she smiled back and then the tram moved on with a big advertisement on the side saying

BOVRIL

and the ad on the back saying Nugget Boot Polish as he watched it rattle away and went about his business which was the maintenance of gas lights in a dun-coloured Drumcondra. And he remembered her and her pretty face until he died and now they're buried . . . pretty girl and stranger both . . . too much to hope for that their graves lie side by side.

They put a green thing like the top of a pool table over Myles's grave and I walked away. Away off among the crowds of graves, past O'Connell's round tower the arrogant fucker to the entrance and my car outside. The rain pissed down, drenching me and washing all the colour out of the place so that I felt like I was walking through an old sepia photograph and the images of folks long dead and gone around me.

The old man in his bowler. And the child in that weirdly shaped pram. Images . . . all around me. Kids with hoops and boxcarts, frozen forever at their play. A solemn little girl with ringlets, silently watching, waiting. A small boy in bare feet. Two suspicious men in an alley with a barrow. What are they selling? Buying? Stealing? Are they burglars or gun-runners? The last of the Fenians? Or secret agents of the Empire?

It hardly matters

Now.

11

'I THOUGHT YOU were never going to leave that place', said Patrick Pearse. As we left that place. 'I never saw a man eat so many cherry buns at one sitting. Does that wife of yours never feed you?'

'Course she does', I replied, guiding Patrick across the busy Grafton Street, feeling that he might not be used to heavy traffic. ' 'Course she does, suckles me every night.'

'Hah', said Patrick in contempt, looking with some slight bemusement at the price of cashmere sweaters in the window of Brown Thomas.

'Of course Anna feeds me', I persisted in my loyal manner. 'Does a very good spaghetti bolognese, Anna does. Eating it is like Linguaphone. You speak Italian perfectly afterwards. Bloody amazing.'

'Amazing', said Patrick Pearse, unimpressed.

'Yes,' I continued remorselessly, 'let me tell you that like all fat women Anna is an excellent cook and as a consequence we rarely eat out, thereby saving money and doctors' bills. Though we did once go to an expensive restaurant. Funnily enough on the very evening of Myles's funeral. To mark the occasion like. Would you like me to tell you about it?'

'Not here. Deirdre of the Sorrows is waiting.'

'So she is, Patrick', I agreed, hurrying him along towards the Allegro. 'And we all know that no woman likes to be kept waiting for anything . . . except maybe an orgasm.'

Patrick sighed, but said nothing. By now, I realised, he had got used to my vulgarity. Like bread off a duck's back thrown by a short-sighted child in Stephen's Green pond . . . it was . . . to him.

Into the car with us, click-clunk with the safety belts, and onwards towards Coolock. Like Mecca, Medina, a Holy Place, like the birthplace or deathplace of some prophet, it shimmered in the distance. We could see it in our minds, Patrick Pearse and I, and we knew it to be strange. Stranger far than Qum, where your glum-eyed Ayatollah broods. And stranger far than far Bihar where bare-shouldered brown girls dance, their bodies a-jangle with bangles, a-quiver with shivers of jewels. Yes . . . Coolock was a shimmering vision to Patrick Pearse and I. And we cherished it, the vision making the journey shorter, the hard road softer, and the journey bearable.

Onward . . . through Mountjoy Square, crumbling, full of despair and the ghostly voices of deceased members of the Irish Georgian Society howling through blind windows of dead houses at raggedy tramps who shuffled past towards the HQ of the Vincent de Paul.

Onward . . . along Dorset Street, tumbling, full of despair and cheap furniture shops and grandiose public houses and disintegrating buses advertising beer . . . good cheer . . .

Onward towards the far off dream world of Coolock. Through Drumcondra now, land of takeaway fried chickens and bedsitter girls from Termonfeckin wearing chainstore uplift bras and regretting it . . . land of canals and litter and railway tracks . . . place of lonesome culchies trying to find their way home from Croke Park, looking up tiredly at advertising hoardings, searching for answers and finding only another question.

What's a Guinness between friends?

FUNLOVIN'.

LAUGHIN'.

VOMITIN'. Take your pick . . . and shovel too and travel on, past Home Farm Road, Griffith Avenue, Collins Avenue . . .

'I knew them well,' said Patrick Pearse, 'Griffith and Collins both. Fine men . . . in their own way.'

'Never met them,' says I, 'but I knew Home Farm . . . now there was a patriot . . . there was a patriot . . .'

Past roads and avenues of dark nineteen-thirties semis, all pebbledashed and castellated . . . little palaces where day follows day as the pubic hair grows grey . . . where dust gathers in that little Holy Water font inside the front door, unused since Vatican Two. This is De Valera land. In these quiet houses the occupants huddled fearfully, reading Dublin Opinion, as

German bombers thundered overhead, thankfully on their way to bomb Liverpool. This place is neutral. Three-wise-monkey land.

Onward . . . past a hole in the road surrounded by men who are dressed in boots and jeans and the jackets of suits from forgotten weddings . . . they're having a tea break, reading The Mirror and The Star. On page three if they can count that far they'll find a photo of some naked English trollop with fat lips who some deranged journalist in mercifully far away Manchester has decided to describe as The Daughter of A Colonel in The Household Cavalry . . .

She'd make us stand to attention any day, eh lads?

Nudge nudge.

Wink wink.

Wink wink suddenly went the brake lights of the cars in front. And then they stopped. And we stopped behind them.

'What NOW', said Patrick Pearse irritably, 'why are we stopped?'

'Traffic jam. Too many cars on the road. Not like your day eh? Suppose you could call this the triumph of the revolution. The lowliest peasant gadding about with four wheels under his ass.'

'Revolution has nothing to do with motor cars.'

'Try telling THEM that', I nodded towards the lowliest peasants in the cars about us. 'They'd sooner lose their balls than their Fiat one two sevens.'

'Perhaps,' remarked Patrick wisely, 'perhaps the two things have become overly synonymous. Perhaps modern man is suffering from misplaced virility.'

'Oh yes,' I agreed, 'that he indeed is. The very phrase. Misplaced virility. That's what Anna says to me whenever I CONFESS that what I really want for Christmas is Serena O'Boyle.'

'WHO', asked Patrick Pearse, as well he might, 'WHO on earth is Serena O'Boyle?'

'She's the Lolita of Glenageary.'

'What's a Lolita?'

'Oh. Well. A Lolita is a young one with slender limbs. A dream. Almost a fantasy. Every middle aged chap like me has a Lolita. Mine is Serena O'Boyle. She lives down the road, smiles knowingly as I pass in the Allegro . . . confusing me so much that I try to change gears with my prick.'

'What happens?'

'What do you think. The gears grind, that's what happens.'

'But that doesn't EXPLAIN. What's a Lolita? Someone you lust after?'

'LUST? LUST? Not a bit of it. No common or garden word like lust can define the relationship between a male menopausal and his Lolita, NOTHING can define it.'

'Well what is it then?'

'It's . . . it's . . .' I searched for words in the far back alleys of my brain. 'It's . . . it's . . . it's just that I want to savagely rip the flimsies off her and lep up on her with a primaeval roar.'

'Oh,' said Patrick disapprovingly, 'I see.'

Not sure whether he did or not, nonetheless I lapsed into silence and thought. I am a modern man . . . and the traffic jam my cloister. A place of quiet thought and introspection. And the beeping horns my Angelus. Aaahh . . . The Lord never demolisheth one monastery . . . but He buildeth a six-lane highway in its place.

'Aaahh,' I said to Patrick, delighted with this perhaps Joycean turn of phrase that came into my mind, 'Aaahh, The Lord never demolisheth one monastery . . .'

'What are you on about?'

'Let me finish. But he buildeth a six-lane highway in its place. Neat, eh? Neat.'

He looked at me suspiciously. 'What do you MEAN, Martin O'Shea, what do you mean? Please try and be more explicit. You have a woolly mind. Who taught you English essays in school?'

'Brother Fintan.'

'Well he has a lot to answer for.'

12

A FRENZIED BEEP of horns behind told me that the traffic jam was over. Now if there's one thing I can't abide, which there isn't, there are many things I can't abide, but if there's one thing that gives me the sick it's traffic beepers. If God had meant me to be a New York taxi driver he'd have given me a bullet proof screen at the back of my head and a jewish mother who'd escaped from Warsaw in '38 now living on the wrong side of the Cross-Bronx Expressway.

So. Beepers. Give me the sick. I turned about and made a rude gesture at the car behind, only to feel my two fingers go limp as I realised that the car behind was full of two big men in bulging sportscoats with an aerial sticking out of their roof. I gave them a friendly wave.

'That car behind,' I said to Patrick, putting my foot down, 'it's the Special Branch . . . do you think they're following you?'

'Me?' He turned about nervously. 'Why would they be following ME?'

'Well you're a subversive, aren't you? A desperate man . . . who'd stop at nothing . . . maybe they think you're planning to hatchet a sub-postmistress to death for the pension money.'

'Poppycock', muttered Patrick, looking warily behind. 'Look, they're going off down there . . .'

And so they were. Relieved, I whistled merrily as we rattled along, the prospect of spending the afternoon in the Lubianka of the Bridewell getting thumped by heavies as I helped them with their inquiries had given me quite a turn. Patrick Pearse too; though, instead of whistling, he started to grumble.

'The city's falling to bits', he grumbled as we entered Santry, on our right the Swiss Cottage Pub which I thought was in London and to our left a large field full of mechanical equipment for sale or hire, their buckets and shovels and scrapers high up in the air like claws.

'It's ALWAYS been falling to bits,' I said, 'it's just that it's bigger now ... there's more of it like ... to fall to bits ...'

'I blame the Act of Union', said Patrick. 'That was a shocking thing altogether.'

'Shocking,' I agreed, 'but in my opinion the rot set in long before that. The third Milesian Incursion was the turning point.'

'It certainly changed things', agreed Patrick.

'Nothing's been the same since', I concurred. And, as I concurred, the traffic lights turned green and I set off down Coolock Lane. My heart was heavy and I thought it time to lighten the gloom in the car with a little humour.

'I say I say I say', I said. 'Patrick did you hear about the Provisional IRA traffic lights, the ones they set up in Free Derry when they were in control?'

'No, Martin,' he replied, carefully, 'tell me about the Provisional IRA traffic lights?'

'Well ... so obsessed were the provos with the need to erase the memory of all things British that they re-designed the traffic lights. Green for GO. Green for Be Ready To Stop. And Green for STOP. Ha ha, isn't that funny?'

'Not overwhelmingly so', he observed.

'Perhaps you're right.' The grin slid off my face and fell into my lap and sat there like a child crying.

* * *

Coolock Lane winds wendingly through ancestral fields.

Strange quasi-countryside, this oasis here, deceptive to the ill-informed who might assume ... indeed who might PRE sume that he had arrived in rural parts at last. That the long grey night of the decayed city was over ... that he was back in God's green world of brown eyed cows, hedges a-squawk with birds, ditches a-run with lesser mammals furry, darting about on skinny legs, long snouts a-twitching ...

In Coolock Lane.

Patrick Pearse, ill-informed, out of date and who could

blame him, sixty years is a long time in town planning, Patrick ooh-ed and aah-ed at the rural scenes about us.

'This is the real Ireland', he remarked.

I said nothing.

Drove on, around another corner. Patrick looked ahead expectantly, assuming that, no doubt, around this other corner his eyes would be regaled, his spirit refreshed with some new rural delight. Like maybe a comely buxom milkmaid, sitting on a three-legged stool, milking a buxom cow, the buxomness of the two females forming a symbiotic synthesis of Mother Nature's bounty, of the RIGHTNESS of all things, of God's republic come to dwell on God's own earth, an earth awash with the running milk of breasts, the running feet of children and the laughter of a contented population, so to speak.

We wended on, with Coolock Lane, around another corner . . .

And suddenly there we were on the Oscar Traynor Multi-Lane, Bi-Lingual and Dual-Carriage Highway. There we were looking down across a flat and featureless plain of grubby little houses which, like an encampment of huns or visigoths on the rampage, stretched away into infinity. No words could describe Coolock.

'GOOD GRIEF', said Patrick Pearse.

'There's no good about it,' I put in, 'this is grief pure and simple. That grey lump over there is the Northside Shopping Centre, this is Coolock and, on the horizon on a clear day you can see Legoland.'

'Oh Dear', said Patrick. As well he might. 'Oh dear . . . I had expected it to be . . . well . . . different . . . a little village.' He paused grumpily. 'It used to be. In my day', he added bleakly.

'A LITTLE VILLAGE? Get up on your horse, Paddy, this is the twilight of the twentieth century . . . this is your industrial revolution, man . . . I'm telling you . . . that piss-willy little revolt of yours only succeeded in knocking down O'Connell Street . . . this here is the REAL THING . . . what did you expect . . . a nation of strong young men and comely maidens?'

'Something like that.'

'Dancing at the crossroads? Jesus you're worse than Donncha O'Dulaing . . .'

'Who's he, never heard of him?'

'Don't you get RTE in The Beyond? No, suppose you don't. Well Donncha O'Dulaing has a radio show in which he travels around the country interviewing the soul of the nation. In pubs and GAA halls. They play fiddles and remember who was left full-forward for Roscommon in twenty-six.'

'Who does?'

'THE SOUL OF THE NATION. The soul of the nation wouldn't be seen dead without a fiddle in his armpit, a pint in his left fist and a fragmentation grenade hanging out of his crios.'

'You're a cynical man, Martin O'Shea', said Patrick Pearse.

'ME? A cynical man? Not a bit of it. Sardonic, I may be. Sarcastic, most likely. Bitter, perhaps. Tired, definitely. Addicted to strong drink and tipped cigarettes, usually. Obsessed with breasts, sex and the more peculiar brands of women's underwear . . . naturally. Overweight and underworked . . . yes. Suffering from a variety of anxiety-induced neuroses and a melange of physical symptoms pertaining thereto, ranging from a simple tic in the left eyelid to hardening of the arteries, not to mention elevated blood pressure, dizzy spells, in-grown toenails and a grumbling ulcer in the duodenum . . . . YES . . . all that . . . but CYNICAL? Patrick, you do me an injustice.'

'Oh for God's sake,' interrupted Patrick, 'do stop going on and on . . . can't you see I'm depressed?'

'Alright alright', I said, not too cheerful myself. I pulled the car in alongside the shopping centre.

'Why are we stopping?' Patrick asked.

'Well where do you want me to go?' I waved my hands about dramatically . . . 'that way? Or over there? WHERE? Where does this bird whatshername live?'

'Emily Farrell. I don't know . . .' He looked desperately around. 'The place is so BIG.'

'Well you would have thought you'd be better organised than this, Patrick, I mean this is a bit Irish isn't it? Here we are, ten o'clock in the morning, in the middle of a housing estate infested with the lower orders, tens of thousands of the buggers . . . . Jesus Christ . . . we haven't a hope in hell of finding this Emily Farrell. And . . . if we don't find her . . . kabush . . . no Deirdre of the Sorrows.'

'Don't be pessimistic, O'Shea . . . is it any wonder you're

still a clerk in the ESB if that's your attitude to life?'

'Stop sounding like my mother-in-law. Anyhow . . . it's not that I'm pessimistic . . . it's just that we're wasting our time . . . we haven't a hope in hell of finding her.' I looked out the window gloomily. 'NOT A HOPE IN HELL' I solemnly intoned.

'Well let's just wait here a while', said Patrick Pearse.

'Lookit,' I insisted, 'just LOOKIT. We'll never find her and there's absolutely no point in hanging round this kip.'

'Martin,' he said sternly, 'if there's one thing I've learned about you in our mercifully short acquaintance it's that you are almost invariably WRONG.'

'No I'm not,' I protested, 'I'm quite often right. Quite often. As a matter of fact in 1973 I successfully predicted the winner of the Grand National. Much against the advice of my wife, mother-in-law, colleagues in the office and blokes in-the-know in pubs. I backed the winner and if I'd had the courage of my convictions beyond fifty pee each way I'd be a rich man to-day. A rich man. Like Paddy McGrath.'

'Who?' said Patrick, not much interest in his voice.

'Paddy McGrath. He's a leading Irish industrialist.'

'Never heard of him.'

'Jesus you're really out of TOUCH, aren't you? Imagine never hearing of Paddy McGrath. I suppose you've never heard of Tony O'Reilly either? Well he's in beans, basically, baked beans . . . though he does own the Irish Independent newspaper along the way.'

'It's been a long time', mused Patrick, a trace of wistfulness in his voice. 'A long time. Whatever happened to the Murphy family? They owned the Independent in my day. Remember them well. Figured prominently in the nineteen thirteen strikes and lockouts.'

'Presumably not on James Larkin's side?'

'No. The Independent was all for starving the workers into submission. Not to mention shooting the leaders of nineteen sixteen out of hand.'

'Well I see their point. We must never bow down to terror or the rule of the gun in the hands of the lawless man who has no respect for democracy anyway. Read that in The Irish Times the other day. It's their leader number 12A. Whenever there's another atrocity they trundle out No 12A, dust it off and print it there beside the letters to the editor from Mary Robinson and other activists in the vanguard of social progress. Letters about contraception and Wood Quay . . . Jesus Patrick, come to think of it, you're lucky you're not buried in Wood Quay . . . . . .'

'Why? Why am I lucky?'

' 'Cos they'd be putting an office block on top of you, that's why. Though in your case I'm sure they'd compromise a little . . . leave your shin bone sticking out from under the foundations or something . . . as a gesture . . . they're great for the gesture that lot.'

'Sometimes a gesture is all that is needed', said Patrick thoughtfully.

13

WELL WELL WELL, here we are in Coolock and still no sign of Deirdre of The Sorrows, no sign at all. Just the dreary coming and going and to-ing and fro-ing of tired looking housewives dragging small children in their wakes like little multicoloured rowboats bobbing behind sad ships that'd seen better days. Nice little cheeky-eyed children, all dressed in nylon clothes from Taiwanese sweatshops what have put our native sweatshops out of business thus emphasising the simplicity of international economics which can be likened to keeping the floor clean by sweeping the dust under the rug.

'No rickets here,' I mentioned, 'thanks be to God. We've come a long way since.'

Patrick did not answer. I tried again.

'The future of a nation is its children', I declared.

Patrick disagreed. 'The future of Ireland is in its ancestors', he opined. 'Every journey has a beginning and an end. Unless we know where we're coming from . . . we'll never get to where we're going.'

'The past is another country,' I quoted, 'they do things differently there.'

'Piffle', said Patrick, neatly placing the works of L. P. Hartley in proper perspective.

Obviously this line of conversation was only heading towards Doheny and Nesbitt's pub and the same place again please no leave me out ah go on but the wife is waiting let her wait it's a woman's role give this man a pint or will you have a short yes a short I think now what were you saying about the ruination of the country there's your man from RTE what's his name can't remember neither can I paid for nothing those buggers hanging around pubs your woman's got a fine pair of who won the three thirty I didn't hear but the going was soft so that rules out Jockstrap.

Obviously this line of conversation was leading nowhere so, anxious to know a little more about Patrick and what enlightenment he could give me on the saorstat of affairs so to speak, I tried a different tack . . .

'Tell me, Patrick . . .'

'Yes?'

'Tell me about how it was . . . like how did you FEEL . . . say when they were taking you out to be shot?'

'Well I wasn't very pleased. I wasn't too happy about the way things had gone.'

'That's understandable. I wouldn't fancy being put up against a wall myself.'

'Well . . . not so much that . . . I'd always expected that to be the end result . . .'

The blood sacrifice bit?'

'Precisely. But it was the intervening events . . . or should I say the LACK of intervening events . . . it was that I found upsetting.'

'How do you mean?'

'Well, you must know. You're an educated man. Up to a point.'

'Thank you, Patrick.' I nodded gratefully for the minor compliment, pleased that the Christian Brothers' efforts with the chair leg across the back of my neck had not totally been in vain.

'Thank you, Patrick . . . but I don't . . . really . . . know . . . what you mean.'

He sighed, wearily . . . as if about to explain some abstruse point of Irish grammar to a tardy kid in St Enda's school at five thirty in the afternoon at the end of a long day with the rain coming down over Rathfarnham from the mountains cold and hard and bitter . . .

Wearily, Patrick Pearse sighed . . . and then he spoke.

'There is, I will admit, something rather incongruous about the leader of a revolution arriving by bicycle. But that is how I did arrive, Willie and I pedalling along the quiet deserted streets that Monday morning.'

'What was the weather like?'

'Sunny. Calm.'

'A good day for a blood sacrifice.'

'Quite. Quite. We cycled to Liberty Hall, to meet up with Connolly, get ourselves organised . . .'

'What did you think of him, James Connolly?'

'A most efficient man. During the course of the subsequent fighting it was he, I will admit, who kept up any semblance of organisation at all . . . a most efficient man . . . one feels, however, that his aims and mine were not necessarily the same.'

'That's putting it mildly. Your man wanted a workers' republic.'

'Yes. A workers' republic.' Pearse spoke the words slowly, distastefully, as if expressing his opinions about some vulgarity or another.

'A workers' republic. Yes. Indeed. But I felt that our differences could have been ironed out later . . . if all had gone to plan . . .'

'Sure they would have been. Connolly would've had you lot shot . . . Stalin wouldn't have been in it if your man had taken over.'

'Perhaps perhaps. There would definitely have been some sorting out. A power struggle, what have you . . .' Pearse smiled gently . . . 'but do not necessarily assume that the ICA would have been the winners.'

'The ICA . . . the Irish Countrywomen's Association?'

'The Irish Citizen Army . . . you fool.'

'Sorry. These initials always bug me. I never know the difference between the SDLP and the PFLP . . . the only thing I know is that the initials usually stand for words like progress or democracy or freedom while the guys in the organisations stand for something entirely different.'

'True perhaps, true. So, as I mentioned, I cycled into Liberty Hall to meet Connolly and the others. Little did I know then, as I parked my bicycle against the railings, little did I know that not long afterwards the same Liberty Hall would be bombarded by the gunship Helga.'

'Britain rules the waves.'

'Indeed. In those days anyway.'

'Yes. Poor buggers are down to their last rowboat now. The Queen's going to use it to escape when Britain finally goes down the plughole. I think myself she'll go to New Zealand. They'd like her there.'

'I've nothing against royalty.'

'Well YOU wouldn't, would you Patrick? You have a touch of the royals yourself . . . sorta aloof and distant. AND, as a matter of fact, I have nothing against the British Royal family myself. I'm very fond of those duchesses and princesses who are distant cousins of the Queen. See them opening things on telly. I look at them, cutting the ribbons to open up some damn polytechnic or home for battered wives . . . look at them and think . . .'

'What?'

'Well I'm sure you don't want to hear what I think.'

'Not particularly. But I like a man to finish his sentences.'

'OK. I think . . . as I look at them . . . I think to myself . . . is your duchess or princess there wearing a frilly black suspender belt under her nicely cut Norman Hartnell clothes? And are her breasts round, ovoid, pendulous or firm and high like a schoolgirl's. There. I knew you wouldn't want to hear what I think.'

'Not when it's such lewd and tasteless meanderings, certainly not.'

'Well. I'm a child of the times. And these are lewd and tasteless times. Look out there . . . at Coolock . . . look . . . do you see anything there that wouldn't drive you straight away for solace into the nearest woman's bed? Dammit. I'm only a breast fetishist 'cos of the failure of modern architecture and town planning.'

'Hmmm.'

'OK. Go on . . . go on with your story. You got to Liberty Hall . . .'

'Yes. And things started to go wrong immediately. My sister Mary Brigid came rushing in and said "Come on Pat, leave all this foolishness."'

'That must've been embarrassing. For a revolutionary leader. In front of all his men.'

'Certainly was. A bad start. Well. So then we marched on the GPO, a ragtag army if you ever saw one. The populace ignored us, only taking an interest in The O'Rahilly's fine motorcar which puttered along with us. And then, at the GPO, we found out that we'd forgotten the flags.'

'Sounds like the Marx brothers.'

'Marx? Did he have a brother?'

'Different family. Carry on.'

'One Karl Marx certainly strikes me as being an ample sufficiency. As they say. Yes. Anyhow . . . we sent runners back to get the flags, hoisted them up on the top of the GPO, the golden harp on green, and the tricolour.'

'Still there, the tricolour, fluttering away, intimidating the British Home Stores to keep its distance . . . reminding us that we are a nation . . . once again . . . fluttering away in the gentle breeze of freedom, over the busy city as it bustles about its business. Aaahhh . . . O'Connell Street . . . I love it . . . every inch . . . the wise old statues, the nuns in Clery's, the doorman outside the Gresham checking your American passport before he lets you in . . . love it . . . love it . . . the starlings in the trees . . . the lights in the trees at Christmas . . . the gurriers in the trees on St Patrick's Day howling down "get them off ya" at the big sturdy American girls who march in the procession with their big naked thighs that'd crush you to death if you were lucky . . . love it . . . love it all . . . right down to the last formica topped table in the last half abandoned Italian chipper . . . . right down to that wino sitting on the seat under O'Connell's angels muttering exhausted obscenities at typists' legs as they pass with their apple and bag of crisps and Jacob's club milk biscuit in their little hands for lunch . . . love it . . . my place . . . my city . . . I am happy here . . . the bones of my ancestors for a thousand years under my feet

as I walk on by

around the corner.'

'Are you quite finished?' asked Patrick Pearse in an irritated tone.

'Surely. Sorry. Got carried away. Drunk with words. Carry on . . . by all means . . . please do . . .'

'Where was I? I seem to have lost my thread.'

'In the GPO. The flags up and all set to go.'

'Yes. Next we built a barricade across the street, so we could cut across and down to Amiens Street Station.'

'For a quick getaway?'

'Not at all. To keep in touch with our outposts. We built this barricade but dammit every time it was up the citizens would rush out and steal it.'

'The BARRICADE? They stole the BARRICADE???'

'Yes. Hard to credit really . . . I mean what earthly use is a barricade to anyone?'

'Usefulness has nothing to do with the urge to steal . . . I remember well the Case of The Wooden Leg in which a two-legged man stole a wooden leg and found himself up before the District Justice about the matter. Well the DJ made a few relevant . . .'

'I don't want to hear about the Case of The Wooden Leg.'

'Sorry.'

'Alright. What I was saying . . . it was understandable, if reprehensible, understandable when the populace came out later on in the fighting to loot the damaged buildings . . . understandable, I mean to say . . . they were poor people . . . in need . . .'

'Oh they understood alright. You guys were sort of keeping nix while they were ripping off stuff.'

'Why must you always see the worst in everyone? The inherent nobility of man would surely be a better facet to dwell upon.'

'Oh I agree. It would indeed. Indeed. But you see personally I'm hung up on Original Sin . . . the FALL, all that bit. That's just me. You see philosophies . . . in MY opinion . . . are much like pairs of shoes. If they fit nice and snug . . . wear them. But anyhow . . . tell me about yourself . . .'

'Well. We took over the GPO and waited . . . preparing our defences. Though as a matter of fact it was Connolly and Collins who organised the military end of things. I prepared my speeches . . . took notes . . . and contemplated the magnificence of it all.'

'No better man.'

'Hmmm. Then, around one o'clock, the first shots were fired. A company of lancers charged up O'Connell Street on horseback, waving their swords . . . a splendid sight . . . even though they were the enemy . . . they reminded me of the Fianna of old . . .'

'Not the Fianna of Fail?'

'Certainly not.'

'What did you EAT, by the way, in the GPO?'

'Well the Cumann na mBan organised a canteen. We sent detachments out into the shops to requisition supplies. Gave them receipts promising compensation from the Irish Republic.'

'That must've gone down a treat.'

'Hmmm. Shopkeepers can't see beyond the quick profit.

But . . . .'

'Yes, Patrick?'

'Let us not waste time talking about shopkeepers. Or prattling on about long gone fighting which is amply documented. Perhaps I may quote from my last letter to my mother. In which, and now I quote, I said "We have done right. People will say hard things of us now, but later on they will praise us".'

'Yes yes. Very true. Your memory won't die for the lack of praise.'

'And that is all that matters. To be remembered. As I once wrote . . . "I care not though I were to live but one day and one night provided my fame and deeds live after me".'

And with that he lapsed into silence. And I looked about and thought my thoughts. And sure enough . . . sure enough . . . in the wistful world of grey Coolock his fame and deeds lived after him. In grey towns everywhere his spirit speaks.

Remember who you are
as time blows by.

14

THROUGH MANY CIGARETTES I sat in silence, every so often turning on the car radio, listening for a moment, turning it off again. At that time of the morning there is a current affairs programme which never seems to cater for my affairs, either current or past or future. And worse, the linkman on that programme has an unfortunate delivery . . . piled up upon which he is usually discussing other people's unfortunate deliveries, the programme being aimed at a certain female audience
  But not at females that I know
  Hosanna
  Praise The Lord
  My own hosAnna has a minimal interest in breech births. Cerebral Palsy she can take or leave. The Woman's Political Association leaves her bewildered and distraught. Consumer Affairs are much less interesting than her own. And she thinks that the Problems of The Underdeveloped World have something to do with flat-chested women
  And perhaps they have
  For all I know.

* * *

On and on the linkman blattered, with each fatuous comment trying to outdo the one that went before. And usually succeeding. On and on I waited . . . for Deirdre of the Sorrows. And when she eventually did come I was so tired of waiting, watching, expecting, so tired that I would not have seen her if

Patrick Pearse had not suddenly said
   'LOOK . . . There she is . . . AT LAST.'
   It was her. And she moved with dancing footsteps.
   As if, coming along that litter-strewn pavement towards the car, it were as if her feet were remembering last year's games of hopscotch . . . games that she was just too old to be playing now. But only just.
   She looked fourteen . . . but I guessed her to be an undernourished fifteen, sixteen at the most. She wore blue jeans . . . painted onto her skinny legs . . . just the merest hint of female curves about her hips . . . and around her waist a belt which said:

jeans jeans jeans jeans jeans jeans jeans jeans jeans jeans jeans.

On her top she wore a white tee-shirt which looked as if it had been washed in the other detergent. And she had no discernible breasts. If she had . . . I would have noticed. I notice breasts.
   Instead, in the positions in which one day no doubt the breasts would appear . . . such being the way of things . . . for which much gratitude to The Lord . . . in those positions she wore two large and shiny plastic badges, each approximately two and one quarter inches in diameter, one a garish coloured photograph of a young man whom I assumed to be in the music industry, and the other a drawing of a lunatic smiling sun with the words "Nuclear Power – No Way!"
   Above then . . . my initial impressions of Emily Farrell.
   Hoppitty-skip, almost a child, but not quite . . . hoppitty-skip, almost an adult, but not yet . . . she came closer. I now noticed that her height was in the region of five foot one and two-third inches. That her hair was blonde. That this blonde hair of hers reached, almost . . . but not quite . . . to her shoulders. And that, as she hopped and skipped, little locks and little strands of this blonde hair fell continually over her right eye.
   These things I noticed.
   Also . . . I saw that her fingers, the fingers that she used to brush away this hair from in front of her right eye, the fingers were very thin, very slender, very white. As was her face, white, heart-shaped, high cheekbones . . . and large blue eyes which

matched almost perfectly the colour of her jeans.

Enough. No further observations were necessary. Emily Farrell was a very pretty girl. And she looked, because of grim Coolock all round us, she looked even more beautiful than the beautiful girl that she was. A flower in the wilderness does not necessarily have to be very special. The fact that it is a flower, and it is in the wilderness, that is enough.

Hoppitty-skip, hoppitty-skip, she came closer still. And now on her feet I noticed that she wore flip-flop sandals of the type that one might buy in Woolworths or the British Home Stores. And how her toenails were painted:

yellow green pink blue red . . . yellow green pink blue red.

This, I must admit, this I found disturbing.

'So that's her, eh', I said to Patrick Pearse as she drew level with the bonnet of my car. 'So that's her. That's Emily Farrell.'

'That's her,' he agreed, 'that's Deirdre of the Sorrows.'

'Hmmmm,' I murmured thoughtfully, 'you sorta don't expect to see the famous Deirdre with yellow green pink blue and red toenails.'

'Why on earth not?'

Well. To that I had no answer.

The girl drew level with my open window. She stopped, crouched down slightly, peered at me and said, in an accent that would open a can of Heinz baked beans . . .

'WHAT THE FUCK IS GOING ON HERE?'

* * *

I opened the front passenger door, patted the vinyl seat invitingly with the palm of my left hand. Emily Farrell, shaking her head in a 'get him' expression, slid in. Her jeans rasped across the vinyl. Elaborately, she crossed her legs.

'So who are you', she asked, that same unpleasant can opening accent which contrasted so shockingly with the perfection of her lips.

'Martin O'Shea. I'm an ESB executive.'

'Jasus. Bet they never turn YOU off.'

'If I didn't pay my bill they would. The ESB is very FAIR.'
'Shower of fuckers.'
'Well they're that too. Depends how you look at it. Anyway, what brings you here, Emily?'
'Well', she said, then paused, thoughtfully, biting her lower lip with her top teeth and looking at me out of the corners of her eyes. 'Well . . . let me put it this way . . . did you ever see the film Close Encounters of the Third Kind?'
'About flying saucers?'
'Yes.'
'No. I never saw it.'
'I bet you did. You're trying to be difficult. May I call you Martin?'
'Surely.'
'Right. Martin. Do you realise that you look like John Travolta. From a certain angle.'
'Good God.'
'Seriously. Older though.' She grinned. Her teeth were lavatory bowl white. 'A lot older . . . any how . . . that's got nothing to do with it, has it?'
'Nothing at all.'
'Right,' said Emily, 'I was coming home from the pictures. We were walking along, a big gang of us. Eating chips, kicking cats, annoying people at bus stops, you know the scene.'
'Right.'
'Well. There I was. Minding my own business. When I hear this voice in my head. A woman. Saying her name was Deirdre and she has something she wants me to do for her.'
'What did you say?'
'I thought I was drunk.'
'You don't mean to say you DRINK at your age?'
'I'm fifteen and a half.'
'You're only a child.'
'JESUS. Do I look like a child?' Saying this, Emily made certain adjustments to her posture which I suspected were intended to demonstrate her minimum curves to the maximum advantage.
'Yes', I said, ungallantly.
'Well bugger you. 'Cos I'm not.'
'Alright. You're not a child.'
'People my age are MARRIED in Africa.'

76

'Bullshit.'

'They are. I read it in a book. Married, or carried off into harems for oul' fellas about seventy.' Emily made a face. 'Yeech', she added.

I smiled weakly. It seems she could just as easily have said 'oul' fellas about thirty-two'.

'Well?' I inquired, in an effort to hurry her up, get her off the subject of child marriage and onto more relevant things. 'Well?'

'Well . . . this voice in me head went on and on, yapping and nattering like. On and bloody on. Even when the boyfriend was kissing me goodnight in the bus shelter . . . there she was, Deirdre, making rude comments about his acne. As if he could help it.'

'Very unkind of her.'

'Yeah. Very off putting too. There he was . . . putting his hands up my jumper to get a feel . . . you know the way fellows are . . . of course you do . . .' Emily Farrell giggled . . . 'You're a fella too.'

'That I am', I admitted.

'Yeah. Anyhow. Shocking off putting. The poor eegit fiddling with me tits and there's Deirdre inside my head saying things like "I wouldn't stand for that if I were you . . . it's so undignified" And me trying to concentrate but giggling instead. She can be shocking funny, Deirdre can.'

'I've heard she has her moments.'

'Yeah. Anyhow. I got in home. And there she still was, nattering on about Alba which is what she calls Scotland and how she lived there with these three fellas having a great time of it until this wicked old king got everyone killed 'cos he DESIRED her himself and she died of a broken heart it was sad really like how these two trees grew out of the grave her three fellas and herself were buried in and the two trees sort of intertwined and then your man the wicked old king had them chopped down but they grew again.' Emily drew breath, sighed heavily, looked sad. 'Certainly a romantic story. Like do you ever read True Story Romances?'

'Well I can't say I do.'

'You should. Romance is a lovely thing. It's such a cruel world. But anyhow . . . Deirdre's story makes True Romance look sick SICK LIKE SICKO.'

'Well I suppose it would. Particularly the way you tell it.'

Emily looked at me carefully, eyes narrowing, nose twitching, as if I smelled unpleasantly. Nervously, trying to remember if I'd applied my BRUT deodorant in the rush that morning, nervously I held my arms tight against my sides. To prevent further offence.

BUT . . . it was not that I smelt. Her expression, I realised, her expression implied that she was THINKING. And what she was thinking was:

IS THIS GUY TAKING THE PISS OUT OF ME?

How did I realise this?

Because . . .

Emily said . . .

'Are you taking the piss out of me?'

'Now why would I do that?' I asked, the innocence spreading over my face like white snow on a dark street in a blank slum. 'Why would I do that?'

'Because you're a clever jerk, aren't you? With your fancy car. I bet you enjoy taking the piss out of the working classes. Well look here let me tell you mister . . . .' Emily folded her arms, sat back in the seat and adopted a Marxist-Leninist expression which sat ill upon her pretty features. 'Look here mister let me tell you I'm PROUD to be a member of the WORKING classes it's people like me who keep you in your fancy car with your posh accent doing nothing but EXPLOITING your fellow humans we're all HUMANS you know in God's eyes didn't he say blessed are the humble and it's easier for a camel to pass through the eye of a needle than it is for a rich man to enter the kingdom of heaven what do you think of that . . .?'

'Well I don't think much of it really Emily,' I confessed, 'myself I'm a member of Fine Gael and in actual fact I think the working classes should be sterilised or at least put into special camps out of mischief. How do you like that?'

Emily's eyes widened, her mouth fell open and she paled. Yes most perceptibly, she PALED . . . 'Oh . . . . Oh . . .' She spluttered, 'Oh . . . Oh . . . you big bollicks how DARE you.'

I shrugged non-commitedly.

'How DARE you?' she repeated. 'Well let me tell you my daddy is a shop steward in the Irish Transport and General Workers Union and if he heard you say that he'd kick your face in.'

'Well let's hope he doesn't hear me then.'

Emily stared at me. Her blue eyes bubbled with hate. Her chest rose and fell with the heaviness of her breathing.

I stared at it. Her chest. Trying to catch a glimpse of those tits which her boyfriend had been groping. And all I can say is well the lad must've had a damn sight better eyes than me.

'Stop looking at my chest, fascist.'

'Surely you mean "chauvinist"?'

'You know what I mean.'

'Oh.'

It seemed, not to put too fine a point upon it, it seemed that, at this moment in time, as no doubt Emily's dad would have expressed it, at this moment in time we were, Emily and I, in a confrontation situation.

At an impasse.

And then suddenly, as I decided that, that we were at an impasse, suddenly I heard old Patrick Pearse, reappearing in my head.

'Martin,' he said, 'I say I say I say . . .'

'Yes Patrick?'

'I say I say I say . . . . there were these two Pakistanis, travelling along a mountain road. In the Himalayas.'

'Yes?'

'Travelling along, chatting away. Getting on great guns with each other. Well . . . suddenly they came to a fork in the road. And one of your Pakistanis . . . well he wanted to go one way . . . but the other, he wanted to take the other fork, right?'

'Right.'

'And they had a long argument about it. Got quite heated in fact. Nearly came to blows. Until, the older, the wiser Pakistani, he held up his hand, said look here Abdullah . . .'

'ABDULLAH?'

'It's a Pakistani name.'

'Sounds more Arab to me.'

'Stop nit picking. Anyhow. He holds up his hand, says look here old chap . . . it's no use arguing about it . . . let's face it . . . this argument is not going to get us anywhere. Do you know why?'

'Why?'

'BECAUSE WE'RE AT A KHYBER IMPASSE.'

'Good God.'

'A KHYBER IMPASSE,' roared Patrick, almost deafening me, 'A KHYBER IMPASSE . . . isn't that terrific?'

'Terrific', I said. And closed my eyes.

15

EMILY FARRELL LOOKED at me with eyes that were big and blue and beautiful. Not soft, nor hard neither, nor anything in between. Merely alive, the waiting and primitive eyes of a creature only half-domesticated, a creature that might, at any moment, revert into primal savagery, go berserk . . . and eat me.

'I thought you'd fallen asleep,' she said, 'your eyes shut like that.'

'Not a bit of it', I replied, carefully. QUITE carefully, in fact. Emily Farrell, I reckoned, needed careful handling. The femaleness of her nature, the ignorance of her brain, the politics of her shop steward daddy . . . all combined to create an explosive mixture, to be handled with EXTREME CARE, transported like dynamite from place to place under military guard. If she fell into the wrong hands there was no knowing the damage she could have caused.

'Not a bit of it, I was just thinking.'

'You wouldn't want to strain your brain,' she chirruped automatically.

'Precisely. Now. Tell me more. You're in this bus shelter, your boy friend is feeling your tits . . . . carry on from there.'

Emily looked down at herself, at the imaginary mammaries, thought for a moment. 'Well . . . let's see . . . didn't I get past that bit. Yes. I was at home. In bed. Deirdre was nattering on to me, complaining about the posters on the wall and saying things like if I thought they were real men then I needed looking at. Like how I should've seen Naoise and Allen and Arden. They were REAL fellas. Tall and straight as young pine trees and all that bit. Real heavy stuff.'

'Who the hell are Naoise and Allen and Arden?'

'The sons of Uisneach, you eegit . . . her three fellas . . . she went to Alba with them.'

'Oh yes', I said, remembering my mythology. 'What did she need THREE men for anyway?'

Emily giggled. 'Well you know the way it is. I read in a book like how one WOMAN can satisfy a HUNDRED men one after the other and ask for more. Like. But it doesn't work the other way around, does it? A man is knackered after one good . . .'

'Alright, Emily,' I interrupted, 'I get your point.' I looked at her, she grinned cheekily at me. 'Incidentally, what sort of books DO you read . . . what's all this garbage about the marriage habits of Africans and now the sexual capabilities of men and women?'

'Jesus them's smashing big words.'

Hmmmm. I thought. I always do that when I think. I hmmmm. Also, when I read, I mouth the words. Which is not really relevant, other than to reveal that the motor functions of my brain are most probably stuck in some pre-puberty stage of development. Perhaps that's why I'm obsessed with breasts and married Anna. And perhaps the reason SHE has those enormous yokes is that SHE is suffering from some glandular malfunction. Yes. It all hangs together. We are slaves to our chemical processes.

SLAVES . . .

But I think I've drifted off the point, i.e., I hmmmm when I think. So I hmmmed. And thought . . .

There is more to Emily Farrell than meets the eye. She is a clever little brat. She is taking the piss out of me. This I do not like, this cannot be allowed to continue. I am a member of the middle classes, part of the AAA readership of the Sunday Independent, I have my dignity. Which, at all times, must be stood on firmly. Lest it wriggle away like a many-legged creature from under a stone and vanish.

So. I stood on my dignity.

'Now look here, Emily', I said, a serious expression on my face. 'Now look here, why don't you just tell me what you are doing here in my car, why you came here, how, in fact, how you knew that this was my car and I wasn't just some potato crisp merchandiser totting up his orders prior to going into Northside to fill up the racks with salt 'n' vinegar, chipsticks, peanuts and funny-bunnies.'

'What the hell are funny-bunnies?'

'I haven't the remotest idea. Just made it up. Sounds like something kids eat.'

'I don't. I never eat convenience foods.'

'You don't?'

'No. Never. Not ever. My daddy says it's a capitalist plot.'

'Potato crisps are a capitalist PLOT?'

' 'Course they are. You see the capitalists train the kids to eat junk at an early age so's when they grow up they won't know the difference and they'll be stuck with junk for the rest of their lives. That's capitalism. That's what my daddy says. There won't be peace and harmony until all the capitalists are shot.'

'Hmmmm', I mused. 'Must meet your daddy some day.'

'You wouldn't get on', said Emily, with remarkable prescience. ' 'Cos you see you're a class traitor.'

'A class traitor?'

'Yeah. You're not REALLY a poshie, Martin O'SHEA, anyone can see that. You're just pretending to be. REALLY you're one of us.'

'ONE ... OF ... YOU ...?' I said in deathly tones.

'Yeah. I bet your old man was a builder's labourer or a brickie's mate or some class of a shit shoveller.'

'MY FATHER,' I said, 'my father was a GENTLEMAN. He bought his hacking jackets in Callaghan's of Dame Street, was a member of the RDS before they admitted people from Dundrum, drank morning tea in Mitchells and took off his hat to ladies both in and of the street.'

'OH YEAH? Well what did he do? For a living?'

'DO? What did he DO? GENTLEMEN do not discuss what they DO. That's what makes them gentlemen. It's immaterial what a gentleman DOES ... you silly little flat-chested scrubber you.'

At which, to MY HORROR, Emily Farrell burst into tears.

Her face crumpled up, looking suddenly like an abandoned piece of paper on the pavement outside a chipper in the cold light of morning. Her face crumpled, her shoulders heaved, tears trailed down her cheeks and great sobs belched up from her innards.

It was a shocking sight to see.

Particularly as it was my fault. I felt terrible. I felt as if I had run over a blind nun on a pedestrian crossing or been caught exposing myself outside a girls' school ... not that I know precisely HOW I should feel if either of those catastrophes should befall me . . . but a chap has a pretty good idea.

'Come on, Emily,' I said, stupidly enough 'let's not have a scene.'

I reached out one tenatitve hand to console her. The way one does, somehow imagining that physical contact will create a bond of understanding and thereby vitiate whatever unpleasantness has precipitated the tears in the first place.

I reached out one tentative hand to console her. It was a mistake. For, as my consoling fingers settled lightly on Emily's shuddering shoulder, she reacted violently, hurling herself backwards away from me, curling herself up into a small untouchable ball like an introverted brillo pad.

'Don't TOUCH me. Don't you DARE touch me.' She said.

'OK', I agreed, withdrawing my consoling hand and placing it on the steering wheel beside its companion. Nervously my fingers stroked that lambswool steering wheel muffler which, in some mad moment in an auto accessory shop, I bought. Along with an aerosol can of QUIK-Start, a sham-chamois and a little feeler gauge for setting one's points and plugs accurately to within one milli-millimetre thereby saving fuel and THEREBY cutting down one's dependence on Arabs whom I hate.

Yes. Everybody has to hate someone, just as everyone must love someone. For the mental health. I love myself, my wife, my daughter and all other women in that order. And I hate Arabs. Therefore I am in equilibrium. Which is better than being into librium.

Yes. Incidentally the reason I WENT into that auto accessory shop . . . normally I wouldn't be seen DEAD in such a place, those guys in rally jackets with 'ELF' or 'FIAT' on their epaulettes, those guys give me the willys . . . BUT . . . the reason I went in was to investigate the price of a new battery as Anna had been complaining about pushing the car to start it every morning even though I told her she needed the exercise to firm up her muscles and she shouldn't let herself to go seed she still complained. So off with me to buy a new battery.

Until I saw the price.

'Are you MAD?' I said to the guy in the rally jacket with 'FIAT' on his epaulettes, 'ARE YOU MAD?'

'It's got a two year guarantee', he mentioned.

'HAH,' I riposted, 'two year guarantee is it. Well let me tell you straight off that I don't believe in guarantees, two years or otherwise. EVERYTHING I buy, young man, every SINGLE thing I assume to have a guarantee, whether stated or otherwise. I have made it my business to read the Consumers Protection Act and, on slightest provocation, I will SUE.'

'Suit yourself', said the lad, shrugging his emaciated shoulders and wondering if he had the nerve to hit me over the head with a tyre lever. He hadn't. And I didn't buy the battery.

'Come on, Emily,' I said, 'what's the matter? I mean I know you're under strain. But we're all under strain. This is an unusual situation we find ourselves in, you with Deirdre of the Sorrows and me with Patrick Pearse. It's an unusual situation, but let's not let it get us down. Let's face up to it, square our shoulders and . . .'

'Oh shut up,' she interrupted, wiping her eyes with the back of her hands, 'you talk too much.'

'Well . . .'

'SHUT,' said Emily, 'UP.'

And so up I shutted, waited, watched as the girl, with fingertips now, carefully wiped away smudges of eye make-up from her cheeks, peering into the vanity mirror on the rere of the sun visor which came with the car at no extra cost along with the push button radio and other incidentals too trivial to mention or even remember when one is halfway through the long months of HP payments, mechanical breakdowns and the soaring cost of petrol.

(Fuck those Arabs anyway.)

'I'm sorry I cried,' said Emily, 'I'm alright now.'

'Good', I said, risking that one word even though I'd been told to shut up and it's my policy to always obey a direct order from a female no matter how inconsequential either the order or the female may appear to be. The truth being that such appearances are always deceptive. Because females are never inconsequential due to the fact that they have wombs and must be cherished as the mothers of future generations yet unborn as my mother told me at an early age and her opinions being repeated, intimated and re-inforced by the opinions of other women whom, during the slow progression from fumbling adolescent learning the intricacies of bra straps in the back seats of cinemas to mature male fully confident and eager to spread his seed far and wide as dictated by his genetic programming for which much thanks to God and much admiration for His Plan or to cut a long story short:

Hold women in Deep Respect and Awe and they will take their own clothes off.

When a bird tells you to shut up. Shut up.

Be sure and confident that a woman's anger will, with the logic of a stream that gurgles over rocks down heathery hillsides to the slow meandering plain below, the once turbulent water becoming miraculously a placid pool where flowers float and ducklings dabble, with that same logic a woman's anger will soon turn into something else. Laughter, love, lust or the urge to possess a spin dryer, whatever. The point is women only have one emotion, one urge, one basic NEED. All is subservient to this basic NEED, all she says may be interpreted as an expression of this NEED, no matter if she speaks in Babylonian patois of the architecture of ziggurats, no matter if she speaks in a Mount Merrion accent of the problems of battered wives, no matter if she says things, strange things like 'equal pay for equal work', 'the living room needs a new carpet', 'mine's a vodka and white', 'chauvinist pig', 'I have a headache', 'the price of meat is only ferocious', 'my ambition is to travel', 'you never loved me anyway', 'I'm sick and tired, d'you hear, sick and TIRED', 'no thanks, I'm on a banana diet', NO MATTER . . . no matter what she says. It can be all summed up in one sentence, what she is really saying is:

I NEED TO BE LOVED.

Understanding this makes life simple. And simplicity, above all, is to be cherished. Particularly in a world of microchip processors which . . . and mark my words . . . will only bring SORROW.

Yes. Mark my words.

It is WRITTEN.

So. Realising that simplicity was to be cherished I decided that the best thing to do for all concerned was for me to love and be nice to Emily Farrell . . . even though as a nymphet she fell some distance short of the standards set by the great Serena O'Boyle, the wide eyed and high breasted Lolita of Glenageary who, every weekday morning, FLAUNTED herself on the station platform before us glum ranks of sex-crazed commuters.

BUT . . . despite all that . . .

I decided to love Emily Farrell. A flat chested bird in the car . . . is worth two tits no matter how firm and succulent on the opposite platform.

So.

'Good', I said.

'Good what?', asked Emily, looking at me threateningly.

'Good that you're alright now. That you've stopped crying.'

'As if you care', she said, with a little residual sniff to remind me that, if I wasn't careful, she'd burst into tears again.

I was careful, saying nothing, content to sit there silently rubbing my fingers on my furry steering wheel and looking out the window at folks going in and out of Northside Shopping Centre with supermarket trollies which, or so I have been led to believe by notices, in supermarkets, cost thirty pounds apiece and are not to be removed under any circumstances as they are there for the convenience of all customers and fair's fair and we're all in this together and let's try and make an effort to pull ourselves up by our bootstraps now that we're in the EMS because believe you me once that starts to bite supermarket trollies will cost around four hundred pounds each and will be chained to the wall like collection boxes for the Augustinian Missions on bar counters. And THEN you lot can bloody well hump your handipacks of coal home on your backs like your fathers and their fathers before them and think yourselves lucky you're not chained to the wall like Augustinian collection boxes and be BLOODY GRATEFUL that you have coal brought all the way from Poland at vast expense for YOUR BENEFIT when your parents had to do with wet turf and cardboard shoes and nothing between their backs and the elements but a collarless shirt and a brown scapular. Think yourselves BLOODY LUCKY that the government have the economy well under control and things can only get better or worse or stay the same and in any of these eventualities it won't be the government's fault because after all they'd be only too happy to jack it all in because it's no fun really just say the word but don't say you haven't been warned when some Workers Party are putting you all up against the wall in the tradition of Workers Parties elsewhere we could mention like Cambodia or closer to HOME across the water to our partners in Europe we'll say no more about it.

JUST WATCH IT.

Keep your head down. Be careful, say nothing. Be content to sit there silently rubbing your fingers on your furry steering wheel and looking out the window at folks going in and out of Northside Shopping Centre with supermarket trollies.

'OK. OK,' she said, 'now I'm OK. Now where was I?'

That question I took to mean that I could now speak again, that she had released me from my vow of silence. 'Well,' I tried to remember, 'well I think you were in bed with your posters on the wall and Deirdre telling you that your pin-ups were awful looking schmucks.'

'Yes. Though she'd never use a word like that.'

'Probably not. I got it from Kojak. It's Jewish. Yiddish. Schmucks. Guys in delicatessens in Manhattan say it to each other. As a matter of fact . . .'

Emily interrupted, silently, holding up the palm of her right hand like a traffic policeman fresh from training school or a citizen about to swear an oath that at the time of the crime he was nowhere in the vicinity and that, as a matter of fact, there wasn't a SHRED of evidence against him other than concocted by a brutal police force and if he was convicted then Hibernia and Magill magazines both if not The Irish Times would want to know the reason why, governments would fall and the judge's wife would have her kneecaps drilled off with a Black 'n' Decker.

'Ssssh,' said Emily, 'don't you START again.'

'OK OK'. I folded my arms across my chest, zipped up my lips and tilted my head inquiringly into its listening position.

She looked at me carefully, much as one looks at a dog one has told to 'sit', making sure that I was obeying the order before proceeding. Satisfied, she began.

'I couldn't get to sleep with her going on and on, complaining about the bedroom and me and Coolock and everything and saying well if this is my reward for being one of Ireland's leading historical figures then it was a poor kettle of fish it only goes to show. And I said lookit Deirdre I didn't ask you to come into my head and if she was so bloody fussy then why hadn't she gone to Foxrock or somewhere where women wear headscarves and have horses. And Deirdre laughed and said most of them looked like horses too but in any case she had no choice and no control over the matter. And at least I was pretty if not beautiful and that made up for a lot of things because contrary to what ugly women say beauty is much more than skin deep. It goes right through and comes out on the other side. Just the same as ugliness. So any HOW . . . .'

Emily sighed, took a deep breath, uncrossed her legs and stretched them forward. Not at all sure what this gesture was supposed to be for I stared thoughtfully at her crotch and the way her jeans cut into her like an axe chop in a tree.

Emily then, with wriggling movements, carefully inserted her hand into the pocket of the jeans and extracted with no little difficulty a squashed packet of ten Major cigarettes and a box of matches.

She opened the packet and took out two crumpled cigarettes, put one between her lips and handed the other to me in that most characteristic gesture of her social background, i.e., with the tip pointing towards my forehead and the rest of the fag firmly clenched between thumb and two fingers.

We lit up, settled back for a moment blowing smoke at each other and doing untold damage to our health but it was our decision and we made it and that's what living in a democracy is all about.

'So any HOW,' said Emily, breaking the total silence in which the cigarette transaction had ensued, 'so there she was, going on and on. Until I lost my patience and said look here OK but like what's all this about?'

'What did she say?'

'She said patience child, everything comes to she who waits. Don't worry 'cos I'll just be around for a few days to get my bearings like and then on the twenty-second of June I want you to go down to Northside Shopping Centre at ten o'clock in the morning and there, parked outside, you'll see a red Allegro car and a man in it waiting.'

'So what did you say to that?'

'I said lookit that's all very well but I have a job sticking pricetags onto cat food in the supermarket and if I don't turn up then I'll be out. There's hundreds if not thousands waiting for that job what with youth unemployment and I only got it 'cos Daddy is a shop steward carrying on sensitive negotiations with the retail sector about the conditions of the staff toilet where you wouldn't put a pig.'

'And what was her answer to THAT?'

'Well she went all huffy and said LOOKIT. Lookit when the angel came to the Virgin Mary with the message you'd all be in a right mess if Mary had turned around and said come off it if I get pregnant what'll people say. You've no idea how people talk in a small place like Nazareth.'

'Hmmm. Not really a fair analogy, in my opinion.'

'What's an analogy?'

'It's something you get from washing powder, on your hands. Or from pollen. Like in hay fever, that's from an analogy. As a matter of fact you can have an analogy to anything. Some people have an analogy to cats. Brings them out in hot lumps and the gaspers, cats, it's the furriness of the buggers.'

Emily looked at me carefully, her eyes narrowing dangerously. 'You're taking the piss again, aren't you?'

'Yes', I admitted.

'Why are you such a big bollicks?'

'I have no idea.'

'Were you always one?'

'A big bollicks? Yes. I suppose I was. Even when I was little, I wasn't a little bollicks, I was a big bollicks. Funny, isn't it?' I grinned amiably at the child.

She stared at me intently, her face experimenting with several gestures and discarding each until she settled for a sardonic smile. 'Tell me,' she murmured, 'how much did those false teeth cost you?'

The bitch. She'd hit me at my weakest point. Not that my teeth are false, but they look it. And many's the time I had considered having them out and getting real false ones that looked real. Dentists can do wonders these days.

The bitch. Carefully I prepared my riposte. Something about the way her ribcage protruded through her grubby tee-shirt might do nicely. But it was not to be. My rapier-like wit was pre-empted . . . by forces greater . . . .

16

'NOW LOOK HERE . . .', said Patrick Pearse, suddenly reappearing like a grumpy bear coming out of hibernation and not liking the look of things outside his cave. 'Now look here . . . this is all very well and good but if you two are going to sit here squabbling and bickering like children all day then it's just a waste of time and a poor kettle of fish all round.'

'I QUITE agree,' put in Deirdre of the Sorrows emphatically, 'believe you me life is short and it behoves you to make it sweet as possible. I can't abide time wasters, shilly-shallying, procrastination or argument for the sake of argument.'

Well . . . Emily Farrell and I, faced with these two aggressive personalities . . . well . . . we just sat there looking at each other, neither quite sure of the next move. Not that we had to be. Patrick and Deirdre had it all sewn up.

'I say, Deirdre,' said Patrick, 'I've just had a jolly good idea. Why don't we get out of this awful place and go climb the Sugarloaf Mountain or something. It's a lovely day. Great view from up there. Great fresh air, clears the old head.'

'That's a smashing idea,' she agreed, 'yes let's do that.'

'Right', said Patrick. 'Come on, Martin, make a move, man. We haven't got all day.'

'But', I started, only to be hushed immediately by Deirdre.

'Don't argue with your elders, young man, do as you're told. This minute.'

'Yes Deirdre.' I started the engine of the car.

If Patrick Pearse wanted to climb the Sugarloaf Mountain then, my asthma, rheumatoid arthritis and lumbago notwithstanding, then we would climb the Sugarloaf.

And so, to that end, I pointed the car in the requisite direction. No matter that we would now have to cross the city again, no matter that I was paying for the petrol, no matter that it was my nerves that were being frayed by city traffic, my blood pressure that was elevating, my arteries that were becoming clogged by fatty deposits caused by stress, anxiety and the fear of double decker buses . . . no matter . . . if Patrick Pearse wanted to climb the Sugarloaf Mountain . . .

Then the Sugarloaf Mountain we would climb.

No-one could call me unpatriotic.

And so, off across the city again with us. Me driving, Emily Farrell sitting beside me, the safety belt cutting diagonally across her flat chest like a papal decoration, her eyes twinkling as if amused. And Gay Byrne the disc jockey muttering on my in-car entertainment unit.

The man is a saint. The things he puts up with.

But never mind. On across the city. In silence. That is, not talking. Listening instead to Patrick Pearse and Deirdre of the Sorrows having their long postponed discussion.

They had a lot to say to each other.

'Tell me, Deirdre, once and for all,' said Patrick, 'what is your real story?'

'Surely you've read it?' she responded, amazement in that voice of hers which, incidentally, possessed a soft north of Ireland intonation very pleasant to the ears.

'OH YES,' said Patrick, 'I've read it. The trouble is there's so many different damn versions. There's the twelfth century version in the Book of Leinster. Read that as reproduced in facsimile by the Royal Irish Academy.' Patrick sighed heavily, then continued. 'Then there's your fifteenth century version, Death of The Sons of Uisneach. That was edited and translated by Dr Stokes in Windische's *Irische Texte* Part Two.'

'Yes,' agreed Deirdre, 'I liked that version myself. But don't forget that Keating gave another version in his *History of Ireland* in the seventeenth century . . .'

'How could I forget it. And what about the Dublin Gaelic Society's eighteenth century version as published in their *Transactions* in 1809.'

'Eighteen O Eight', corrected Deirdre.

'You're right', agreed Patrick, tapping his head. 'The old memory, you know, not as young as I was . . .'

'None of us are', confided Deirdre.

'Go on with you,' said Patrick, 'you don't look a day over seventeen.'

'Nice of you to say so,' giggled Deirdre in a girlish manner, 'but actually next September I'll be two thousand six hundred and forty years old.'

'WELL', said Patrick, gallant astonishment in his voice. 'WELL all I can say is I hope I look as well as you do, HALF as well as you do when I'm your age.'

'You flatter me, sir.'

'Not at all. Now where were we?'

'At the Dublin Gaelic Society's version?'

'Yes. Incidentally what ever happened to the Dublin Gaelic Society?'

'I'm not quite sure,' said Deirdre, 'did they merge with Gael-Linn . . . you know . . . that bingo crowd?'

'Probably', said Patrick. (I thought I detected a hint of disapproval in his voice at the mention of Gael-Linn.)

'Well,' Patrick went on, 'after the Dublin Gaelic Society's version of your story there was . . . now let me see . . . .'

Deirdre laughed, a tinkling, pleasant sound. 'Surely you haven't forgotten the *Transactions of the Inverness Gaelic Society* in eighteen eighty-seven?'

'Of course. Mr Carmichael's version.'

'Yes,' agreed Deirdre, 'Mr Joseph Jacobs re-told that version in his *Celtic Fairy Tales* as published by David Nutt in eighteen ninety-one.'

'My word you have a marvellous memory.'

'Well', simpered Deirdre . . . (I noticed that she simpered every time Patrick gave her even the merest of compliments.) 'Well . . . I suppose I have . . .'

'You certainly have', said Patrick.

'Good grief,' I interrupted the two of them, 'enough of this mutual admiration society. Let's get on with it for God's sake.'

'Who's he?' asked Deirdre, nodding her head in my direction.

'Martin O'Shea. Don't pay any attention to him. He's moody.'

'Know the type', said Deirdre. And then, with a supercilious sniff, she ignored me. 'So,' she said to Patrick, 'so you want to hear MY version, do you?'

'Fascinated to', he replied enthusiastically. 'From the horse's mouth, so to speak.'

'Hardly the metaphor I would have chosen', put in Deirdre rather huffily.

'Sorry,' said Patrick, 'you have me all confused.'
'OK', said Deirdre. 'Now listen once, and listen well.'

17

'MY FATHER'S NAME was Malcolm. He was a musician . . . a harper . . . harpist I think they call them nowadays . . . any way, he was called Colm the Harper . . . in Irish, of course. By the way, Patrick, would you prefer we talked in Irish?'

'No. I think we'll carry on as we are.'

'Right you be. So. Colm the Harper, the old man, he had a nice little job at the court of King Connachar. Your man was the king of Ulster at the time. And Dad was his court musician, a nice little number . . . something like being a member of the RTE orchestra these days, secure, well paid, union rates, all that bit. None of your one night gigs in Borris-in-Ossory, followed by two weeks on the dole and an engagement in the Irish Club in Luton or somewhere, none of that nonsense. Nope. Dad was very well in there, well set up, nice wife, decent job, well thought of by people who mattered. One's father is very important, that's what I think . . . what did yours do?'

'Well . . . he was actually a sculptor. Took after HIS father before him.'

'Did he really? Was HE a sculptor too?'

'Not a bit of it. Grandad was a picture framer. By trade. But he did spend all his time making bird cages.'

'Bird cages?'

'Bird cages. Carving them out of exotic woods. Intricate little things . . . dozens and dozens of them . . . spent all his spare time at it . . . the artistic impulse you see.'

'I see. And your father inherited this, this artistic impulse?'

'I suppose he did. Though his first job was in a chain factory. Which he HATED. So he left. Took night classes in drawing and then became a sculptor. Came to Ireland in his teens.'

'Oh he was English then?'

'Well I suppose he was. Born in Bloomsbury. I suppose that

makes one English.'

'I suppose it does.'

'Hmmmm. Anyhow. Dad came to Ireland and got a job in Harrison's of Great Brunswick Street. Carving statues for churches, that sort of thing. Funny job, really, for an atheist. But there you are.'

'It's a strange old world. My father, Colm, well as I was saying, he was well off. Had everything together. So to speak. Except that he didn't have any children for a long while.'

'That's hard to take.'

'Very hard. But then, as luck would have it, he met a soothsayer who told him not to worry about it. Though he, the soothsayer, he sorta put it like well I have good news and bad news. The good news is that you're going to have a daughter . . . . and the bad news is that she's going to be the most troublesome young one that Ireland has seen for this long while.'

'That must've shook him up.'

'Certainly did. But not for long. Folks in those days could take the good with the bad. And so, when I was born he arranged for me to be hidden away in the hills with an oul' wan to bring me up. So's I couldn't cause trouble around the place.'

'That must've broken his heart.'

'Not a bit of it. He went back to his harping, forgot all about me.'

'It's a hard old world. MY father James had a lot of problems too. You see because he was an atheist the other sculptors didn't take too kindly to his getting jobs doing sculpting jobs for churches.'

'Shocking. Never approved of closed shops, trades unions, all that bit.'

'Mmmm. Anyhow . . . Dad became a Catholic. To stay in work. Then his wife died.'

'It never rains but it pours.'

'Precisely. But he married again. Soon after. To my mother.'

'That must've been a comfort to him.'

'I'm sure it was. Her name was Margaret, worked in a shop. Only nineteen when she married Dad.'

'A nice age, not too young, not too old.'

'Hmmm. They had four children. I was the second oldest.'

'A nice number for a family. Not too big, not too small. Poor old Colm didn't have any more after me. Though I can see his point. Actually he never even saw me again after dumping me in the hills with the oul' wan. In fact . . . I never saw anyone at all. Except your wan. Do you know something?'

'What's that, Deirdre?'

'I didn't even KNOW there was such a thing as MEN. I was that isolated. Spending all my time wandering around the woods and learning the names of animals and flowers and all that bit. Jesus. In fact I was a bit of a flower myself, sorta slim and slender and, if I say so myself, a rather beautiful bit of stuff.'

'I'm sure you were.'

'You'd better believe it. Some writer described me as a creature of fairest form, of loveliest aspect, and of gentlest nature that existed between heaven and earth in all Ireland . . .'

'Certainly an elegant description. I'm very fond of fine writing myself. Dabbled a bit in it at an early age . . .'

'Did you really, Patrick?'

'Yes indeed. Even wrote plays as a child. The brothers and sisters would take part. Hah . . . had them well organised, that lot . . .'

'I suppose you were their natural leader?'

'No question of it. The brother Willie took everything I said as Holy Writ . . . poor lad . . . didn't have much DRIVE . . .'

'Easily led, was he?'

'That's putting it mildly.'

'Hmmm. I suppose I missed having brothers and sisters. Perhaps my life would've turned out differently. If I had. But there you are. That's the way of it. Not ours to reason why and all that bit . . .'

'In God's hands . . .'

'True for you . . . anyhow . . . where was I . . . yes . . . up the mountain, fair of form and everything and not a twitter of wit on me WHEN . . . SUDDENLY . . . one night . . . out of the blue comes a hunter, knocking on the door of the bothy where I lived with the oul' wan. The poor eegit was lost, petrified with the cold and the hunger and as soon as he arrived the oul wan ate the face off of him. She didn't want him seeing ME, you see . . . 'cos she knew that word would get out. Your man would be off down the mountain to civilisation the next

97

morning, prattling on about this beautiful girl living alone and unknown up the mountains.'

'I know the way it is.'

'Yeah. Sure enough . . . off he went the next morning, after having spent the night staring at me . . . off he went to the King. That's King Connachar, my father's boss. "King," says he, "did you know that there's this most beautiful girl living alone up the mountains with an oul' wan . . . and what's in it for me if I show you where she is?" '

'A mercenary fellow.'

'No doubt about it. But he got his answer. "Lookit," says the King, "lookit here you show me where she is or my executioner will have your head off soon as look at you." WELLL . . . "WELL" said the hunter, "if that's the attitude then you'd better come along." So off with them, the King and a crowd of henchmen, led up the mountains by the hunter and the lot of them arriving outside my bothy in the middle of the night, banging on the door. "Who's that there," said the oul' wan, "it'd want to be the King for me to open up the door." "Well that's just who it is," says your man, "so open up or I'll have this house down around your ears you old bag." '

'Hard times, those.'

'Rough enough. The oul' wan, terrified out of her wits, lept up from the fire where she was knitting an aran sweater or something and rushed to open the door. And in comes King Connachar and all his lads and immediately the poor fellow was smote with love for me. SMOTE. No other word for it. Yarruz, lads, says he to his men, did you ever . . .?'

'And what did they say?'

'I don't know. I was too terrified to notice. There I was who hadn't seen but one man in my life and he the hunter of the night before and now the bothy filled up with this big crowd of sweating warriors, leering at me and looking down the front of my dress and making remarks to each other like you'd hear in a rugby club bar.'

'I've never been in a rugby club bar.'

'But you can imagine . . . things like jasus the tits on your one I wouldn't mind myself she'd do me a power of good mine's a pint what's yours.'

'I see.'

'I wonder if you do but still and all a woman's lot is not a happy one in Ireland, never has been, never will . . . it's the nature of the Celt.'

'Perhaps, Deirdre, perhaps you could proceed . . . with your story?'

'Sorry, Patrick. OK. Well as I was saying there I was being leered at by all these BRUTES and blushing becomingly and all that bit when King Connachar suddenly said in a strange strangulated voice, "That's the girl I shall marry." And with no more ado he threw me over his shoulder and carried me down the mountain to his castle.'

'Well. He certainly didn't hang around, that fellow. Reminds me rather of my own youth . . . once my mind was made up to do something nothing could satisfy me but to get at it right away. I wanted results, you see. Life was short. When myself and Douglas Hyde founded the Gaelic League I was just like that, get right IN, save the language and no damn nonsense or shilly-shallying about.'

'It's the only way . . . I suppose . . . but it certainly was strange for me to find myself at the King's court all dressed up in posh gear with handmaidens and all that. He wanted to marry me straight off but I persuaded him to hang his fire for a year and a day.'

'A wise move. Marriage is one thing you shouldn't rush into.'

'You never married yourself?'

'Dammit woman . . . where would I be finding the time to get married? I was married to my causes, you might say. If it wasn't the Gaelic League it was my studies at King's Inns or my plays or short stories or God knows what . . .'

'But tell me, what did you do, for the year and the day while you were waiting to marry Connachar?'

'Well . . . I did lessons . . . and, to quote one of my biographers, Connachar provided me with merry modest maidens fair who would lie down and rise with me.'

'Mmmm . . . well . . . if you don't mind me saying so . . . that sounds a little strange . . .'

'Well I suppose it does . . . and the things some of those modest maidens fair would get up to when they lay down . . . well . . . it'd curl your hair . . . but life's a strange old place, isn't it?'

'Nothing stranger. Do you know one of the strangest things I ever saw?'

'What was that?'

'Well there was this chap called Owen Lloyd who was a teacher in my school St Enda's for a while. Well he wasn't really a teacher, I suppose . . . but he came in from time to time . . . a sort of visiting professor. Yeats came in too. Not to mention Standish O'Grady. But ANYWAY . . . This chap Lloyd was a harpist and he had the MOST INCREDIBLY LONG FINGERNAILS you ever saw. You'd be sitting there, having a cup of tea, chatting about this and that, and all the while you'd be fascinated, HYPNOTISED by those fingernails, curling around his cup like claws. Very strange. Very STRANGE indeed.'

'Mmmm . . . well I suppose a harpist would need long fingernails for plucking the strings and that. My father Colm, I'm sure he had long nails too.'

'In ancient China everyone but the manual classes had long nails.'

'Indeed they did. But how and ever, Patrick, let me tell you what happened to me then.'

'By all means . . . .'

'Well . . . There I was . . . sitting on a hillock one day with my merry modest maidens fair . . .'

'The ones who would lie down and rise with you?'

'The very same. There we were, sunning our legs . . . giggling and chattering to each other the way young girls are prone to . . . WHEN . . . when over the horizon comes these three lads.'

'Aha . . .'

'Yes. And do you know who they were?'

'Of course I do. They were the sons of Uisneach.'

'The very lads. Allen and Arden and Naoise. Three smashing big boyos carrying swords and shields and all the panoply of war . . . striding along with their big strong legs crashing through the undergrowth and little rabbits and lads like that running helter-skelter out of their way.'

'Ah yes. The beauty of young men in their prime is something that has always affected me.'

'Me too. Perhaps because I lived for so long without them.'

'Well yes. But I would consider that, if I may be so bold, and please don't take me up wrongly Deirdre, but I would consider that to be mere female lust.'

'Would you now?'

'Yes. You see I don't think it possible for a woman truly . . . TRULY . . . to appreciate the beauty of a young man. Because lust gets in the way, dims her senses. So to speak.'

'I see.'

'I wonder if you do. Perhaps . . . and this is only a suggestion, but perhaps if you have a moment some time you might care to visit the National Library and dig up the obituary I wrote for Michael Breathnach who was president of the Gaelic League's college in Connacht and died at an early age.'

'That job would kill anyone.'

'Actually, Deirdre, he died of the consumption.'

'Oh.'

'Yes. A lot of people died of consumption in those days. It was endemic. Not until the infant Irish Republic introduced the free X-ray scheme was it eradicated. Symptomatic, that, I feel, of British misrule and neglect . . . but however . . . let the dead bury the dead . . .'

'What does that mean?'

'I'm not quite sure. But how and ever . . . as I was saying . . . you should read that obituary. If you get the chance. Though, if you have a moment, I could quote a selected passage?'

'Please do.'

'Right you be. Here goes. Quote. He had a figure slender and almost boyish but held erect with what a grace and dignity . . . recall then the kindling red in the pale cheek . . .'

'That was from the consumption.'

'Please don't interrupt.'

'Sorry.'

'Alright. As I was saying . . . recall then the kindling red in the pale cheek, the light in the large soft eye, the spirituality of the whole countenance, the noble gesture of the shapely head with its crown of dark brown clustering hair. End of quote.'

'That's nice.'

'NICE? NICE? Hardly the word I would have chosen, Deirdre . . . Magnificent, maybe . . . STIRRING, perhaps . . . but NICE?'

'Well you know what I mean.'

'Hmmm.'

'Anyway, Patrick . . . we haven't got all day . . . let's get on with it . . . as I was saying . . . there we were, myself and my modest maidens fair, sunning our legs, daringly showing our knees to each other if not thighs in moments of giggling fits but that's neither here nor there ...'

'Quite.'

'God you are a stuffed shirt, Patrick.'

'I have been so described.'

'But I supposed it takes all sorts. Far be it from me to ... OH GOD ... there we were and along comes these three lads, handsome and tall and their legs rippling. With the muscles. Like. So we sort of giggled and waved and held our shoulders back so's our chests stuck out you know the way young girls are.'

'I certainly don't.'

'Well. That was all very whatever. When SUDDENLY, out of the blue, I was SMITTEN, absolutely SMITTEN, no other word for it ... SMITTEN ... SMOTE with love for Naoise, the tallest and strongest and handsomest and most ripplingest muscular of the three.'

'I think "smitten" is correct ... rather than "smote". The latter strikes me as somewhat biblical.'

'You're probably right. Of course you always were a bit of a linguist, weren't you?'

'I did have an interest in language, certainly.'

'Oh don't be so modest.'

'OK. I admit, despite what Father Dineen might have thought, I admit that I consider myself to have been a rather fine linguist.'

'That's better. False modesty is a no-no. In MY book anyhow.'

'That has not escaped me.'

'Hah. I think you're getting at me ... but I'll ignore it. Get on with my story. I was smitten with Naoise.'

'As you mentioned.'

'So I did. Bowled over. Head over heels. So up with me, gathering my raiment about me.'

'Gathering your raiment about you?'

'Right on. That's what Joseph Jacobs the folk story collector said I did. She gathered her raiment about her. Neat, eh? It really means I put on my clothes ... but your man Jacobs was around in 1892 and they didn't say things like that then. They were a bit STUFFED in 1892.'

'I was around in 1892.'

'Oh . . . well . . . yes . . . anyhow . . . I put on my clothes. Not that I'd been naked, mind you, but I'd been down to my flimseys. Like we didn't have bikinis in those days.'

'Thanks be to God.'

'Don't you like bikinis?'

'I think bikinis are one of the most APPALLING inventions of modern times.'

'Ah well I don't know. I often have a peep into Joe Walsh Tours brochures and see all those birds sunning themselves in the Costa del whatsits. Sorta envy modern girls their freedom I mean if you've got it let it all hang out that's my motto . . .'

'I'm afraid you have an unfortunate streak of vulgarity in your nature.'

'Ah get away with yourself. Don't be such a prune.'

'PRUDE, you mean.'

'Prude . . . prune . . . what's the difference? Sometimes I get confused with English. It's only my second language, you know.'

'Would you rather speak in Irish?'

'God no. I find I can't express myself in that language. Like they don't have the words for what I want to say. Like what's a bikini in Irish? There's a for-instance for you.'

'Irish girls shouldn't wear bikinis. So there's no need for the word.'

'Holy MOSES. Irish girls have breasts, don't they?'

'That, reluctantly, I will admit. But it's neither here nor there. Get on with your story. If you would.'

'Alright alright already. Don't be cranky. Where was I?'

'Gathering your raiment about you.'

'Right on. Well. I rushed down from my hillock, screeching at him. Now. Naoise's two brothers recognised me, knew I was the young one lined up to marry the King . . . and knew too there'd be trouble if Naoise got a sight of me 'cos he'd want me for himself. He was that sort of bloke. Strong willed. Impetuous. But his brothers were more cautious. So they rushed him on, ignoring me. But your man, Naoise, wasn't deaf . . . he heard me screeching after him. What's that, says he, what piercing shrill cry is that, the most melodious my ear ever heard. Sure, says the brothers, sure that's only the wail of the swans of Connachar, don't worry about them lads. Don't be kidding me, says Naoise, that's a young one in distress. So he stopped. So we met. And that was IT.'

'IT?'

'Yep. It. We were in love. So he put me up on his shoulder and off with the lot of us to Alba. That's Scotland nowadays.'

'I am aware of that. So . . . you mean to tell me that you ran away just like that?'

'Just like that. You see we had to get out pretty quickly or old Connachar would have had Naoise's head off for running away with his intended. We went to live beside Loch Ness. Never saw the monster, mind you, but we caught the running deer in the woods and fished for silver salmon and all that bit and lived quite happily thank you very much. And Naoise made a woman out of me.'

'A delicate expression.'

'I have my moments. So anyhow . . . there we were, happy as Larry for a while . . . the happiest few months of my life . . . looking back . . .'

'Ah yes . . . we all have them . . . the happiest months of one's life . . . myself now, if I were asked, I would have to say my happiest times were when St Enda's school was going like a bomb in Cullenswood House. Those were the days. Mmmm . . . perhaps it was a mistake . . . but one can never tell, can one . . . but perhaps it was a mistake for me to get ambitious and move to The Hermitage in Rathfarnham in 1910 . . .'

'The bigger premises, you mean? They got on top of you?'

'No, not that . . . but you see The Hermitage had strong associations with Robert Emmet . . .'

'Oh HIM . . .'

'Indeed. Yes. And I think his ghost got to me, his shade was about the place . . . got into my blood . . .'

'Yes. A bad buzz, that Emmet guy. See him around a bit in The Beyond . . . not much though . . . keeps himself to himself . . . don't think he ever got over Sarah Curran . . .'

'The ruination of the man, that woman . . . no offence, Deirdre, but it does seem to me that behind every disastrous life story there lurks a woman's hand . . .'

'I'll go on with my story. Let. Me. See. Yes . . . we were in Alba, having a gas old time of it. But, all the while, worrying a bit what old Connachar was plotting back in Ulster. We didn't hear a squeak out of him. He was biding his time . . . waiting

'. . . the cunning bugger . . .'

'Deirdre . . .'

'Sorr-eee . . . won't use that word again. Anyhow . . . soon it came the time when I was supposed to be marrying Connachar, the year and the day was up. Though why he still wanted to marry me I have no idea. Living with three lads like Naoise and Allen and Arden had sorta blunted my virginity if you get my drift . . . but anyhow Connachar didn't seem to mind. But just to be on the safe side he sent a spy to check out that I was still good looking . . . the spy was a guy called Gelban Grednach . . . arrived in the middle of the night and peered through a hole in the door and saw me. As luck would have it Naoise saw HIM, saw this beady eye peering in and lost his temper, throwing a dice at it. Knocked the eye out of poor Gelban Grednach who fled back to Ireland like a cut cat. Well, says Connachar, how's she looking? And Gelban told him that I was looking so good that he'd gladly lose his other eye to have another look at me. OK. That was enough for Connachar. Inflamed with LUST, he hatched a plot . . .'

'Not a good time to hatch a plot, if you ask me. Lust and logic make poor bedfellows . . .'

'Right on, Patrick . . . but Connachar hatched his anyway. He decided to put it about that he was having a big hooley for all his kinfolk . . . and that if Naoise and the brothers and me didn't come then he'd be most disappointed. Like all was forgiven, come home, that bit.'

'And you believed him?'

'I didn't. But Ferchar Mac Ro and his three sons arrived to tell us that everything would be OK. Now Ferchar Mac Ro was the brother of the father of Connachar . . .'

'His uncle.'

'True. But in those days we didn't say things like uncle. Or aunt. We said he's the brother of his father's second cousin by his first wife three times removed . . . sort of more MELODIC . . . in the bardic tradition . . . if you know what that is . . .'

'I am acquainted with it. You may not be familiar with my Cuchulain pageant which in 1909 we performed in Castle Bellingham on the PERSONAL invitation of Sir Henry Bellingham?'

'No.'

'No what?'

'No I'm not familiar with it.'

'Well you should be. It behoves you to know about the history of your country.'

'What are you talking about? I AM the bloody history of my country . . .'

'Don't say bloody.'

'Stop being a schoolteacher, will you? Jesus I'm glad I didn't go to St Enda's or St Ita's wasn't that the girls' school you ran?'

'It was indeed. Though I never got on so well with girls . . .'

'We all have our problems. But we won't go into that. I'm a bit kinky myself. Don't think I ever recovered from laying down with my merry modest maidens at an impressionable age. Not that I think there's anything WRONG with lesbianism, mind you. I mean to say it's all human life isn't it? And girls' bodies are sorta more NEAT than men's, aren't they? Softer too . . . more curvy like . . . which reminds me about one of my modest maidens fair. Well you've never seen anything like her curves she was like one of these bunches of balloons men sell in the street. But perhaps you don't want to hear about her?'

'Remarkably perceptive of you, Deirdre. Carry on with your story, please . . . you can leave out your ruminations on the seamier side of woman's nature.'

'I wish I could speak like that.'

'If you'd attended one of my schools you could.'

'Right on. But that's the luck of the draw, isn't it? SO. As I was saying . . . Ferchar Mac Ro and his sons arrived in Alba to invite us to Connachar's big bash. Right, said Naoise, always the lad for a party. If he was around these days he'd be one of those blokes who carry a six-pack everywhere just in case. Anyhow. Right, says he, get the oul' currach out and we'll be off. Now hold your horses, says me, I don't think this is such a good idea. You see I've had this dream in which I saw three grey hawks coming out of the south with red drops of blood in their mouths and that sort of dream kind of makes you think. I mean I don't care what people say but I think dreams can tell the future what do you think Patrick?'

'The future is the destiny decided by the past.'

'Yeah. Well. Right on I'm sure. But like I don't find that very helpful. As a matter of fact I don't think it even answers my question. But we'll leave it be.'

'Good. So, tell me now, you were invited to King

Connachar's gathering of the clans?'

'Right. Though let me tell you when I got the invite I felt like the corpse being invited to a wake. If you get my drift. How and ever. Ferchar Mac Ro and his three sons ASSURED us that if Connachar got up to any tricks then he'd have to answer to them. In fact, in Ferchar's own words, he wouldn't leave head upon body in the whole of Erin. Which is as blunt as you'll get. So. Off with us to Ireland, two days in a little bobbing boat and there we were. As soon as we landed we sent a message to Connachar that here we were and let's get on with the party or whatever. Connachar sent word back to hang around just where we were 'cos he wasn't ready for us. There was a house on the shore and we were to use that. So hung around we did.'

'For long?'

'Long enough. Then three HUNDRED of Connachar's warriors arrived outside to knock off Naoise and Allen and Arden and carry me off to a fate worse than death as they say though I'm not so sure having ample experience of both . . .'

'You're rambling, Deirdre.'

'No I'm not. What I mean to say is I have plenty experience of oh never MIND you wouldn't understand. SO . . . three hundred of Connachar's men outside. And the four of us plus the three sons of Ferchar inside. The odds were awful. Treachery, screams me at Naoise, I told you so . . . didn't I say so . . . didn't I warn you why didn't you listen to me I told you so didn't I now look at the mess we're in I told you don't say I didn't . . .'

'I get the point, Deirdre.'

'Hmmm. Well. Naoise said will you ever stop nagging me woman. And out the door with him and the others and laid into Connachar's men and let me tell you the carnage was something shocking. Two hundred of Connachar's men got the chop and not a feather out of my side JESUS they were REAL MEN . . . Anyway . . . Along comes Connachar and says in a rage lookit what you've done to the flower of my army you'll be sorry you've got it coming you buggers don't say you've not been warned. So off with him then to his castle . . .'

'To plan his next move?'

'PRE-cisely. And while he was gone with the remnants of his army we decided to beat it back to Alba 'cos enough's as good as a feast. Little did we know that Connachar has summoned up his head Druid a guy called Duanan Gacha to work some nasty magic on us. Little did we know as we hurried along that at that very moment old Connachar was saying well lookit here Duanan Gacha you've been hanging around this castle living it up for forty years at my expense so now's your chance to re-pay me. Right you be, Boss, said Duanan Gacha, I'll put a wood in their path. And he did.'

'I don't believe in Druid magic, Deirdre.'

'Well most people don't until they've had to hack their way through a magic wood that's sprung up in their path out of nowhere. Like the Congo basin it was . . . but Naoise and the lads just cleaved their way through it, carrying me along on their backs . . .'

'What happened then?'

'Well Connachar saw that the wood bit didn't work so he said LOOKIT Duanan Gacha this is not good enough. Let's have some action around here. OK OK said Duanan. And this time he conjured up a big sea in front of us.'

'I find this hard to credit.'

'That's your problem, not mine. The sea was there, that's all that matters. So we swam across it, on and on and on, but the more we swam the bigger it became . . . and soon we were exhausted . . . and Naoise and Allen and Arden were drowned and me nearly though just at the last minute Connachar said dry up the sea you old fool or Deirdre will drown. So Duanan Gacha dried up the sea. And on the grassy plain then there was the bodies of the three sons of Uisneach and me bending over them with my tears. And all the people came from miles around and stood for a long while and there was a silence more silent than was ever heard. Not a bird sang in all the plains of Ulster and not a blade of grass even whispered. Not a mouse squeaked. Not a child laughed nor cried. In that silence a hen's footstep in the dust of a farmyard would have been like thunder. But there was no hen's footsteps. 'Cos no hen moved. And no blade of grass whispered. And no bird sang. And no man nor no woman moved. No-one moved except King Connachar. And even he moved silently. His footsteps left no mark upon the ground, no trace in the grass of his passing. No crack or flapping from his leather cloak, no sign of his kingship in the faces of the silent people as he passed. Nothing but death. He was King of the kingdom of death. And beside him Duanan Gacha, Druid to the kingdom of death, beside him Duanan Gacha walked, an old man with eyes like stones . . .'

'Eyes like stones.'

'Eyes that saw nothing but shadows. And the different shades of darkness in the shadows. Eyes that never laughed nor never cried.'

'Never laughed, never cried.'

'Like you, Patrick?'

'Perhaps. Perhaps.'

'Or are you the King . . . the King of the kingdom of death? Or are you the druid, the priest of the kingdom of death?'

'I do not know.'

'I do. But it doesn't matter. Let me tell you more . . .'

'Tell me more.'

'Connachar and Duanan Gacha came to the place where the bodies of the sons of Uisneach lay, the place where I knelt weeping over them. And the people about asked him what was to be done and he said bury them. So they dug a big grave and placed the three bodies in it side by side. And I stood there watching. And I said to the men who were digging the grave to make it big enough for me. And they did, obeying me because they were afraid, because I had the shadow of death on me like a dark dress and it blew about my body like twilight in a graveyard on a November afternoon. And when it was ready I lay down beside them, the sons of Uisneach, in the grave. And I died like a candle in an empty room. And the men started to fill in the grave, as if they could bury death with a few shovelfuls of clay . . . but Connachar ordered them to stop, to take me out and bury me alone. So this they did. And went away into their lives, growing old and moody beside their fires, telling their children and the children of their children how it was . . . how they were there when Deirdre died. And what a time it was. In those days.'

'Old men are full of stories.'

'And out of my grave there grew a little tree . . . and out of the grave of the sons of Uisneach another . . . up and up into the air, two little trees growing bigger and bigger until their branches met and intertwined over the empty ground between our graves. And the children of the children of the men who buried us would come, and look, and wonder. And go about

their ways. Agus sin e an sceal. So the story ends.'
'Sin é an scéal. Sin é an scéal.'

18

AND SO AND so and so . . . across the crowded city, churning and wriggling like the guts of a dead horse rotting in the sun, out through the southern suburbs, ever so neat, the houses in rows like graves in a new cemetery so bleak before the yew trees grow . . . through the city and the suburbs and out into the country on the south side of the city we went. And all the while, as I drove, Patrick and Deirdre rattled on with their stories.

Neither I nor Emily Farrell spoke a word. We couldn't, even if we'd wanted to. With those two in the car you couldn't get a word in edgeways. I'm telling you . . . those two weren't short of a word or two; an understandable situation, I suppose. After long years in The Beyond . . . it must be a release to speak again with human voices.

On and on . . . through Bray that town of settled tinkers, madmen from the hilly tribes of Wicklow and lesser clerks struggling to keep up mortgages in squinty semis where their wives stare moodily through lace curtains bought on the drip from Clerys . . . stare with eyes gone dead like Christmas tree lights in the beginning of January when all the decorations must come down . . . stare with eyes that only flicker when the valium or gin is wearing off . . . eyes like faded marbles, lost in the garden, dug up again when the child is grown and gone.

And so with sombre thoughts, through Bray. Not that I wasn't listening to Patrick and Deirdre's yattering, no . . . but I have, through long years as a Clerical Officer in the ESB, I have developed the capacity to concentrate on several subjects at the one time.

On a good day, in fact, I can carry on four different streams of consciousness, listen and partake in two conversations, do The Irish Times crossword, make plans for my luncheon and evolve a sexual fantasy concerning the sixth form of the Dominican Convent in Dun Laoghaire and ALL AT THE SAME MOMENT IN TIME.

This is a very unusual facility that I possess, a facility which, on analysis, reveals that I am either a very GIFTED PERSON or, and this is always possible, a very MAD PERSON. Which one of these revelations be the truth depends on one's point of view, whether one be a psychological follower of Adler or merely one who thinks that Adler has something to do with mouth organs . . . though in actual fact now that I dwell on it I realise that the TRUTH is only to be FOUND in my own OPINIONS because I am ALWAYS RIGHT and EVERYONE IS PLOTTING against ME and it's NOT FAIR but they'll be SORRY because

GOD IS ON MY SIDE.

GOD WANTS ME to run riot through the sixth form of the Dominican Convent in Dun Laoghaire, to spread those silky thighs across those inky-stained and initialled-gouged desks, every single one of those thighs, I mean every single TWO of those thighs, thighs coming in twos, usually . . . where was I? Yes. And whether those silky thighs be slim or chubby, slender or rippling with muscles like the INCREDIBLE HULK . . . slim, chubby, slender, or rippling, those thighs belong to ME.

FOR THIS IS MY DESTINY.

But ENOUGH.

Enough of pandering to my sexual peccadillo . . . (Which, incidentally, very incidentally, is a musical instrument much like the COMMON FLUTE as played by James Galway but different in that it is eight feet long, the little holes what the air comes through are SQUARE and it can only be played by siamese twins with long arms like Mr Tickle of the Mister Men and consequently is very rarely found in modern orchestras and more's the pity as to listen to it is a sight for sore ears.)

Enough. Onward. Out of Bray. (Like a full moon it always affects my mental equilibrium, the tides of my sanity go out and I tend to gibber. In Bray.)

Out of Bray and up the steep hill towards Kilmacanogue and the view of the Sugarloaf our destination past Brennanstown Riding School on the left hand side which by all accounts is a wonderful place to learn to ride though not for me 'cos I have

THE FEAR OF HORSES who are dirty big smelly brutes what will kick your head in soon as look at you.

Up that steep hill, Patrick and Deirdre still nattering, myself and Emily still silent, the engine of the car still humming under the expert guidance of my hands on the lambswool encrusted steering wheel.

Up the steep hill and out along the nice new dual carriageway for which much thanks to the dedicated engineers of Wicklow County Council and let's not forget the lads in the Department of The Environment and also their political masters of several administrations without whose farsightedness none of this would be possible.

We've a lot to be grateful for.

Around the corner and ahead of us now the shimmering road to Wicklow, Wexford, Brittas Bay and summer dunes where oily bodies simmer in the sun ... the lucky buggers.

Not for me the sand or sea to-day, oh no. 'Cos off the road I have to turn, up the Rocky Valley, Patrick and Deirdre nattering, Emily silent ... up the Rocky Valley past strange bungalows all converted, for commercial reasons incomprehensible though no doubt viable, all converted into shops of varying degrees of huxterdom, all selling ice cream and large sliced pans of bread as if that were the staple diet of the inhabitants hereabouts ...

Onwards ...

Onwards and up and up and up and around the side of the mountain, up a precipitous road reminiscent of the Pathan-infested hills of Afghanistan ... one almost expects to see long-rifled tribesmen peering out from rocks, but one doesn't ... One merely sees abandoned JCBs parked in abandoned quarries, dumb sheep and pedestrians of mountainy mien and indefinite destination.

Up and up and at last the top and the long road stretching out in front of us across Calary Bog towards Roundwood and the highest pub in Ireland, the usefulness of which adjective as an advertising announcement for a pub always having failed to impress me even less than the 'oldest' or in fact the 'newest' as applied in similar circumstances. I do not rise to such blandishments. And in a similar manner I do not choke with emotion when overhearing my native country described as having forty shades of green, as being an Emerald Isle or, indeed, as being divided into four green fields in the possession of an old woman, a state of affairs both socially and agriculturally intolerable.

But enough of that.

We now turned left down a winding track and travelled thence for something close to half a mile, turned left again onto a grassy little spot and parked the car. Several other cars were already parked there, the occupants picnicking or playing ball with large inflatable beach balls printed TEXACO which I understand are sold at a modest price on the condition that one also buys a certain quantity of that excellent company's products.

We parked the car. From this spot the mountain itself looked shocking high. And a long way away across the tedious moors. Emily and I, I am sure, would have been quite happy to sit in the car and watch other people making the trek up the mountain. But Patrick had different ideas. The bit was between his teeth. Seeing me hesitate, he broke off his conversation temporarily and demanded that I get a move on. And so, wearily, I got going. Locked the car, helped Emily over the gate, and proceeded.

* * *

Jesus Christ ALMIGHTY . . . the full of my health I hadn't been in since nineteen-sixty-seven.

That mountain KILLED me. My legs ached, my heart thudded irregularly, my brow sweated and the bronicals wheezed like a bagpipes being run over by a bus.

I struggled on, the ordeal made worse by the sight of the nubile Emily hopping and skipping along, the trek not taking a feather out of her. Hopping and skipping ahead, laughing at me, she showed not the slightest respect for her olders and betters not to mention her social superiors.

If I had a horsewhip, I thought, I'd use it on her bottom. Then, I thought, I better not think of things like that, the added excitement might be just that final little straw . . . camel's back and all that bit . . . my heart might finally give out, implode in upon itself with a gluggg . . . and that'd be the end of my existence earthly.

So, silently, thinking nothing, I plodded on. The minutes became hours, and the hours became dreams, each one a reflection of the other . . . time became a roomful of mirrors, and I saw myself reflected at odd angles and I thought I was dying. But I wasn't.

I was climbing the Sugarloaf. I was listening to the long stories of Patrick Pearse and Deirdre of the Sorrows. I was alone with Emily Farrell and the sun and the sky and the view of my faraway city, faraway sea, toy boats chugging and the smell of wind.

Rocks skittered away under my feet. Emily danced like a goat. Small children hurtled past in a downward direction to the clatter of stones and the calls of panicing parents who smiled at me as they passed. Folks on mountains always smile at each other. Folks in asylums do likewise . . . we're all mad together . . . I tried to smile back, being a social animal . . . but the smile wouldn't come . . . the life had gone out of my facial muscles. I was dying from the head downwards, the feet upwards . . . all available life gathering around my heart in a desperate effort to keep it pumping.

The body has its own wisdom.

In a heap at the top I collapsed like a load of old clothes falling off the back of a tinker's cart.

'Are you alright', asked Emily, looking at the view.

'Gggccchh', I replied, 'Gggccchh . . .'

'You smoke too much', she mentioned.

'I grow old,' I muttered to the grass in front of my nose, 'I grow old. I shall wear my bottoms of my trousers rolled . . . dare I eat a peach . . . mermaids on the beach.'

Ah yes. I died with the poetry of the dead T. S. Eliot on my lips.

And is that the end of the story?

Not a bit of it.

Because you SEE . . . I DID NOT DIE.

Through the intervention of Divine Providence and with the assistance of St Jude the Obscure I survived. I suppose that other saints and influences had a hand in the matter too . . .

I recovered and sat up and looked about and listened to the final sad words of Patrick's and Deirdre's sad stories.

And then suddenly there was silence and in it I heard little things unnoticed normally like faraway a bird going tweet and baa-baa sheep and Emily whistling and the shush of wind and it was almost dark and I wondered where the day had gone.

'Well, Patrick,' I prompted, 'GO ON ...'

'That's it,' he said, 'that's all.'

ALL? ALL?

What did he mean, that's ALL?

19

'WHAT DO YOU MEAN, that's ALL?', I said, suddenly annoyed. 'For Jesus' sake, Patrick, do you mean to tell me that the only reason you dragged me up here on top of this shagging mountain was to yap on to Deirdre about your life? That the only reason you arrived from The Beyond was for you and Deirdre to tell each other's stories?.

'That's all', he replied.

'But for God's sake . . . we all know your story already. Hasn't it been shoved in our ears and out our arseholes for the last fifty years?'

'Ah yes,' he agreed, 'but the whole point of a story is not in a story itself, it's in who you tell it to.'

'Oh yes?', I said sarcastically, waiting for further enlightenment on this novel thesis.

'Yes. Like music. Tell me Martin, are you a musical man?'

'No, I hate music and I'm tone deaf with it.'

'I see. But anyway. You will appreciate that the whole point of music is that it must be listened to, both by the player and the playee. To coin a word.' He grinned smugly. 'PLAYEE . . . very modern, words like that.'

'I will agree that that's the whole point of music. Yes yes yes get on with it the sun's going down Anna will be worrying about me.'

'And Daddy'll be worrying about me', put in Emily plaintively.

'You're both wrong', said Deirdre. 'Anna is in Dundrum talking to the wives of company representatives and import-export executives . . . and your father is agreeing that the early morning teabreak be shortened by two minutes and as a quid pro quo the night shift will have an extra four minutes clocking-on time to compensate them for unsocial hours and loss of earnings due to the reduction in . . . .'

'Yes yes yes', I interrupted. A blow by blow account of petty trade union bargaining as reported by Deirdre of the Sorrows was too much for me to take. TOO MUCH.

'That's no way to talk to a lady', said Patrick, gallant as ever. 'Have you no respect?'

'HAH,' I yelled, 'have you no respect for us you bugger . . . dragging us up damn mountains, getting me into trouble at work and no doubt at home when Anna finds out I'm not fishing with Walter and ALSO getting Emily the sack from her job of sticking on catfood labels . . . what about that . . . EH EH EH? What about us?'

'I think you will find,' said Patrick thoughtfully, slowly, 'I think you will find, with hindsight, that the whole exercise will have been worth while. You see, Martin, though Deirdre and I will be hopping off now, and though we will soon be gone and all that will be left of us will be stale words in dead history books, posturing patriots, vulgar statues and homicidal maniacs of low intellect carrying out foul deeds in our name . . . when that is all that is left of us, both you and little Emily will find . . . that it has all been worthwhile.'

'Patrick,' warned Deirdre, giggling in that girlish way of hers, 'don't you dare tell them.'

'TELL ME WHAT?' I shouted, 'you're holding something back.'

'I can say no more', said Patrick Pearse, his voice becoming faint and soft. 'The time that was in it is no longer so.'

'What's that supposed to mean?' I yelled, the slightly hysterical tone in my voice alarming me somewhat.

'The heart is a lonely hunter', said Deirdre.

'What are you talking about?'

'At the going down of the sun,' whispered Patrick, 'and in the morning, we shall remember them.'

'That's Winston Churchill', I screeched. 'What's he got to do with it?'

'Know him well,' murmured Patrick, 'a giant of a man.'

'MAD', I yelled, waving my fists in the air. 'MAD, bloody mad the lot of you.'

'The age of giants is over', whispered Deirdre wistfully. And then, 'Let's watch the sun set . . .'

'Let's watch NOTHING,' I roared, 'let's get this sorted out.'

But my roars and rage were all in vain.

And silence now descended with the coming of the night. And I knew that the voices of Patrick and Deirdre were gone and only remained like the memory of a dream fading fast. And soon they themselves would be gone forever and I would be alone. With Emily.

And she knew too.

And so we watched each other.

And then we watched the sun.

20

WE WATCHED THE sun, sinking in the west. Patrick Pearse. Emily Farrell. Deirdre of the Sorrows. And me.

We watched the sun. And it was pink and the sky looked as if a giant candy-floss machine had exploded over Lucan or Leixlip or somewhere in the west . . . and maybe it had for all I knew.

Anything is possible. These days . . . things are not as they may seem . . . here be ghosts and strangeness . . . anything is possible.

The sky was pink with tendrils of red. And perhaps with the merest touches of burnt umber, a smidgeon of vermilion, a dash of faded ochre. But generally pink, so that the towers of Ballymun, Liberty Hall and similar tall buildings reflected this pink colour and looked like the icing on a particularly vulgar wedding cake in a hotel in Longford Town at three-thirty on a wet Wednesday afternoon just before the priest relations go home and folks settle down to serious drinking, bachelor uncles from outlying rural parishes looking at the bride's bosom and wondering precisely what will happen in the honeymoon hotel in Marbella that night after the candlelit supper when the Flamenco guitarists have gone home with their gear and there is only silence and the sound of the blue mediterranean washing wispily outside the bedroom window on a clear day you can see Morocco.

If you want to.

Though in actual fact it's all sand, homosexual shoeshine boys, donkeys, sand, palm trees, bare-footed girls with big brown eyes, camels, sand, poverty, cheap cigarettes and homosexual advertising executives from Copenhagen and Zurich negotiating deals with homosexual shoeshine boys.

So much for Morocco.

White buildings. Black coffee. Brown eyes.

And pink skies too at the end of the day.

I sat on top of the Sugar Loaf and watched the sunset. I sat on a small round rock. My feet rested on dry grass. This dry grass, heather, mossy things . . . a carpet of substances which obviously thrived in wet and boggy conditions and were now, in summer, only reluctantly dry . . . this carpet stretched for perhaps eight feet in any direction. And to my east, when I looked, I could see the feet of Emily Farrell, resting in a similar manner to mine on the dry grass. Except that hers were bare, she had kicked off her flip-flops and was, at that precise moment, wiggling her toes.

I watched.

Now . . . to make one thing clear . . . I am by no means a foot fetishist BUT . . . watching the girl's slim bare feet wiggling there in the grass . . . WELL . . . I found it disturbing . . . in a sexual manner . . . not to pussyfoot about the bush . . . so to speak . . . I got an erection which, cunningly folding my hands on my lap, I neatly concealed with the expertise of long experience. I get a lot of erections and consequently can handle them pretty well. If I say so myself.

And so . . .

Bored with the blasted sunset over there in Lucan, I watched, positively stared at Emily's feet. And a strange thing happened . . .

NOW . . . for various optical reasons, it's a well known occurrence that when one stares fixedly at an object, after a while one begins to see double. Well I do. And it's nothing to do with drink. It's your laws of optics. Probably refraction. Or something to do with the focal length of the eyeball. But whatever it is . . . that's the way it is. One sees double.

And this is what I did. Saw double. Saw, beside Emily's feet on the grass, another pair of feet, sort of ghostly, shadowy feet . . . they're always like that, these images.

And I thought nothing of it.

UNTIL . . .

I noticed that this other pair of feet was wearing sandals. Roman soldier sort of sandals, leather thongs criss-crossed up the legs as far as the knees.

WELL . . .

I closed my eyes. Hard. Opened them again. Stared at the

feet. Yes. They were still there.

My spinal cord went cold. My erection collapsed with dramatic suddenness. My eyes wanted to close . . . but . . . fascinated . . . like a nose hyponotised by a particularly bad smell, my eyes refused to close or look away. Instead they stared at these ghostly, be-sandalled feet. And then, worse, my eyes started following the legs to which they belonged, then the body, then the face . . . UNTIL . . .

There she was. The pink light of the setting sun shining through her, Deirdre of the Sorrows. No mistake about it. Her clothes. Her face. Her hairstyle. No mistake.

This long-ago lady . . . home from the past at last.

'Emily' I hissed.

Emily turned about, looked at me, a sort of 'yes what do you want can't you see I'm looking at the sunset' expression on her face. But only for a moment. And then her eyes widened, her mouth fell open and she stared, fixedly, half-wittedly at me.

No. Not at me.

At somebody, something, beside me.

Out of the corner of my eyes I looked. Of course I knew . . . just what I would see . . . and I did.

Patrick Pearse himself. In uniform. High shiny boots and a hat which reminded me of the Australian army. His face was pale, angular. He looked tired.

And tiredly he stood up, looked down at me for a moment, nodded like a man one meets on a country road, and walked away. Across the little grassy spot to where Deirdre of the Sorrows sat. She waited for him, then stood up.

Face to face for a while, they seemed to be talking. But I couldn't hear anything. Except my heart going boom-biddy-boom-biddy-boom. And the soft sound of wind across the moor. And the faint buzz of a distant car.

Emily and I, paralysed, stared at this historic pair, like children in a museum. For five, ten, fifteen minutes they stood there . . . perhaps more, or less . . . and then with a suddenness that shocked . . . they took off.

Let me re-phrase that. I've made them sound like aeroplanes.

They drifted off. Upwards. Like people being rescued by helicopter, slowly swaying back and forth, rising the meantime. Except that there was no helicopter. Nothing but the rapidly darkening sky of night above their heads.

Emily and I looked up.

The shades of our important ancestors hovered at about twenty feet over our heads and then, suddenly again, they went. Deirdre of the Sorrows vanishing in the direction of Belfast, Patrick heading east towards Holyhead.

'Come back, Patrick Pearse,' I shouted, 'come back, you can't leave me here . . .'

He drifted away.

'Come back, you bastard . . . you can't leave us here . . . what'll we do?'

He drifted away.

'Oh yes. OK. Go on . . . bugger off. Leave us alone. You're good at that. Stir things up and shag off out of it when the going gets tough . . . right . . . nice and easy . . . nice and easy to be NOBLE, eh, Paddy my lad? Well let me tell you something . . . Let me tell you something,' I roared into the night, 'let me tell you it's not bloody good enough. Not BLOODY GOOD ENOUGH . . . we've got to live here . . . we've got to stay . . . we've got no choice in the matter . . . go on . . . alright . . . go on off back there wherever you come from . . . have a chat with Che Guevara . . .'

He paid no attention to my rantings, drifting, drifting away across the sky. And my anger drifted with him. I shook my head sadly and watched as Patrick Pearse got smaller and smaller and over the Kish lighthouse I lost him. I whirled about, just in time to see Deirdre of the Sorrows disappearing through the power station chimneys at the far off edge of Dublin Bay.

I was sorry to see her go. She was me and mine and I loved her.

* * *

'Jasus', said Emily Farrell. To which, after a pause, she added 'Christ.' Then, a further lengthier pause, 'Almighty.'

'My feelings entirely', I put in.

Emily stood up, stretched herself, slowly walked towards me. And in front of me she knelt down, put her hands on my knees, looked into my face and asked, 'what the fuck was all that about?'

'Search me', I shrugged, nervously realising that the touch of the child's small slim fingers was re-activating the erection so rudely driven away by the ancestral shades. 'Search me', I repeated.

'Stop saying "search me".'

'Sorry.'

'S'alright. Do you believe in ghosts, Martin?'

The question, in the circumstances, was so absurd that I laughed. I mean to say . . . two drowning victims might as well ask each other if they believed in water . . .

'Do *you* believe in ghosts, Emily?' I said, placing a fatherly hand upon the top of her head, stroking in a fatherly manner.

'I don't know what I believe. Fuck it. When I was ten I believed in the Bay City Rollers and look what happened to them.' She laid her face in my lap, her soft cheek perilously close to the painfully throbbing fulcrum of my sexual being.

'What happened to them?', I asked, my fatherly hands now striking the silky neck and slender shoulders . . . the lissom arms of little Emily.

'What happened who?', she murmured, moving her cheek, back and forth across the copper studded, the decoratively stitched, pre-faded, posthumously-shrunk fabric covering of my be-jeaned genitals.

'The Bay City Rollers. What happened them? You said . . .'

'Ah don't mind me. I talk a lot of rubbish. It's 'cos I'm from Coolock. We're all IGGURUNT out there. Or so you think . . .'

'Do I? Did I say that?'

'No but I bet you think it HEY . . .' She looked up at me. Big blue eyes the colour of jeans. Lips of inquisitive perfection. 'Hey . . . tell us about your wife.'

'Wife? Wife? What wife?'

'The wife who's at home minding your six kids while you're hanging around mountains with me.'

'I don't have six kids.'

'Ah . . . but you have a wife. Is she pretty?'

'Of course she's bloody pretty. What do you expect?'

'Jesus you're full of yourself. Do you love her . . .? Fancy her like you fancy me?'

'Fancy YOU? Who said I fancy you?'

' 'Course you fancy me. Isn't that why you picked me up in

124

Coolock?'

'PICKED YOU UP IN COOLOCK?'

'What I said.' Emily opened her wide eyes wide, adopted an APPEALING expression. 'Go on. Tell me about her...'

'Why do women always want to know... about the other women?'

'Aha. So I'm a woman now. Not so long since you called me a flat chested little scrubber.'

'You've changed.'

'Not surprised. With that fucking Deirdre of the Sorrows I don't know whether I'm coming or going.'

'HAH,' I said, 'isn't that the same with the lot of us. None of us Irish know whether we're coming or going. If it's not Deirdre of the Sorrows it's Patrick Pearse or bloody well who knows what... too many stories... we're POLLUTED with stories.'

I looked sourly out over the city. And didn't like it much. 'You know what really riles me?'

Emily, looking up from her activity of poking her forefinger between the buttons of my cowboy shirt and tickling my stomach... 'What really riles you Martin? Tell auntie Emily.'

Ignoring her mocking tone, I told her. 'What really riles me is that Patrick didn't stay long enough to hear the end of the story of Myles Flannery's funeral. Wasn't interested. Self centred bugger.'

'Well don't you worry icky-boo.' Her finger tickled my navel. 'You can tell little me. Who the HELL was Myles Flannery anyway?'

'Myles Flannery?' I looked towards the city. And the little glints of twilight in the gloom recalled his gleaming bicycle. 'Myles Flannery? Sure he was the man... he was the man... ah never mind...'

Emily giggled, rolled over onto her back and lay on the ground.

'He was the man...' Her head lolled to one side. And she was silent.

And the mountain was silent. And in the silence I told her a story right to the end. A very long story. And the sun sank and darkness fell altogether and I rambled on.

And when the story was over I said, in the manner of Deirdre of the Sorrows, 'sin e an sceal... sin e an sceal.' And Emily stood up from the grass and repeated it. 'Sin e an sceal.' And then she burst into song like in the ad what attempts to rekindle our language more dead than poor old Flannery.

'IT'S . . . MORE . . . THAN . . . WORDS . . .'

She sang, arms spread out wide

'IT'S PART OF WHAT WE ARRRRRRRRRR . . .'

Then she came back over to where I was sitting, kneeling on the grass before me. And I rested my fatherly hands on her head, pulling it into my lap where she snuggled. And my fatherly hands quietly stroked her neck and shoulders.

And, after a while, deciding that 'fatherly' is a shocking restrictive adjective for a pair of hands to have to carry about a young girl's body, I abandoned the word. And forgot it. Like an old glove on Christmas Eve when one has peeked into the wife's presents and realised that Santa Claus is bringing a new pair . . . I abandoned the word. And it fell to the grass to be eaten by ants and the insects of the night . . . carried away, letter by letter . . . aaahhh . . . nothing goes to waste in nature.

For nature abhors a vacuum.

It's God's Plan.

God made the world and God made Martin O'Shea. If not in His exact likeness, then in a reasonable facsimile thereof. Each part, each facet, each organ of Martin O'Shea has a precise function to perform in God's Plan. His liver is to cleanse his bloodstream of toxic agents mostly alcoholic and his hands have been specifically manufactured, genetically programmed and evolved over tens of thousands of years for one precise purpose . . .

TO HOLD FEMALE FLESH.

Now who am I . . . who am I to fight God's Plan?

A nothing, that's who I am. A speck in the cosmos. A hiccup in eternity . . . one rivet on one wheel on a train of infinite length that thunders through the endless night. That's who I am.

Like it or lump it.

And so, with such philosophies, galactic in their implications for me not to mention the rest of mankind, with such thoughts I made my decision. Emily Farrell must be made love to. There's no way out of it. Because, like the mountain, she is here. And because, not least of all, because she is at this moment in time in a fellatio situation, her head curiously

rummaging in my lap and her little fingers cautiously unzipper-
ing my zipper. Cautiously, carefully, and determined.
 Yes.
 To HELL with it.
 To HELL with IT . . . whatever IT might be . . . to HELL
. . .
 I WILL make love to Emily Farrell.
 If she ever manages to get that blasted zip open. Mentally
writing complaining letters to Mr Wrangler, I manoeuvred my
legs in a manner calculated to unkink the fabric of my jeans.
Women are the weaker sex, my philosophy . . . they must be
helped, onto buses . . . across the road. . .
 Suddenly Emily seemed to lose interest, looked up at me, her
face a pale questionmark in the dusk. 'Did your wife Anna
really do all those things?'
 I nodded my head, happy at the memory.
 'Sounds like a really WEIRD girl. Really WEIRD like
WEIRDO.'
 'Well,' I said defensively, let no-one cast aspersions at the
beloved, 'well if you were a nurse in John of God's you might
be pretty strange yourself. All those guys who think they're
the ram of the Covenant . . . it gets to you in the end.'
 'Or maybe the luncher she's living with? Maybe it rubs off.'
 'Me? Luncher? On the contrary I feel I bring a touch of
sanity into Anna's life. She needs me. I need her. It's a two way
thing. Like ping pong.'
 Emily looked plaintively away. I knew what she was going to
say. And she said it.
 'No-one needs ME.'
 Aha. AH HA. Quick as a housewife washing a floor with
Flash I gave her the answer to THAT.
 'I need you.'
 'Do you really?'
 'Yes', I nodded, looking meaningfully but one hopes tact-
fully down at my half-open zipper.
 Emily gazed thoughtfully at me for a moment. And then she
smiled. How beautiful she is, I thought
 How beautiful she is.
 How beautiful she is I thought as her silky lips came sliding
down over the top of my penis which . . . incidentally and
purely by the way . . . is shaped remarkably like a German

infantryman's helmet . . . a fact which says little about my penis but a lot about that warlike race Our Partners In The Common Market . . . at least I THINK it says a lot . . . but won't go into it . . . the muddy pools of racial psyches are neither here nor there . . . well certainly not here . . . perhaps there . . . and there is a place best left untrodded by my Celtic feet: the particular electrics of my brain have certain limitations.

How beautiful she is.

With her silent slender shoulders

How beautiful she is as over the top of my German infantryman's helmet . . . shag it . . . as over the top of my penis she placed her lips and they felt like dewy flowers in a wild summer garden not that I have ever felt dewy flowers at dawn in a wild summer garden over the top of my penis but I am a poet at heart and not

Just a Clerical Officer

In the ESB

I am a poet at heart who once said to Anna McClafferty now Anna O'Shea at the Martello Tower in Seapoint your breasts are like moons which sounds definitely poetical

Though she giggled

At the time.

The brat is seducing me, I decided, the words bringing into neat symbiosis the seduction of me by Anna McClafferty by her breasts and now the seduction of poor me by Emily Farrell's lips so indescribably soft and delicate and warm. And if these seductions go on

I'll be a FALLEN MAN and your Ayatollah's followers will throw stones at me in the street

The half-black bastards

Their half-cocked theologies

Really BUG me.

The beautiful brat is seducing me, I realised with my hands now far from fatherly running up under her tee-shirt to the place where her breasts would be when she got older. I don't know why my hands went there, perhaps from force of habit but no matter. Shockingly surprised my hands found that Emily did after all I must be going blind it's the male menopause

Oh My God

She did after all have small definitely definable and soft fleshy protruberances surmounted by fully grown nipples all waiting, as t'were, waiting for the breasts to grow about them and in the meantime . . . waiting for my hands.

Between finger and thumb I rolled one nipple. As if I were making that money-implying gesture beloved of Greeks and other trading peoples mostly greaseball dagoes really but fine folks nonetheless let's remember the Phoenicians and not forget the Parthenon it's not their fault they lost their marbles

To Lord Elgin

I am hallucinating again

It's them mushrooms does it

To the brain.

Between finger and thumb I rolled Emily's right nipple . . . or left, I cannot remember but I don't think it's important . . . nipples is nipples and life is short . . . between finger and thumb I massaged it into a small hard thing reminiscent of or a facsimile of albeit miniature I must add in the interests of Public Relations . . . a facsimile of my own erection now buried deeply in her throat. Some women have the gift of breathing through their noses, a gift from God like beauty or the ability to make puff-pastry . . . you either have it or you don't.

How beautiful she is

I thought

And time passed

And as it passed I looked over her blonde head towards the city and I thought of all the people out there who would just love to change places with me on top of my mountain and soon hopefully on top of my Emily and tough shit to them . . . let them watch the Rockford File instead . . . .

Time passed and eventually Emily surfaced, shaking her hair away from her eyes and grinning a grin of rare strange beauty and saying in her Coolock accent now weirdly blended with the Donegal of Deirdre of the Sorrows

'Jesus that's lovely'

And the words were music to my ears.

21

THE NIGHT HAS a thousand eyes.

But, unfortunately, ESB Clerical Officers only have two. And they're in the front of his head. And, when he is lying, face downwards, on top of a young one who is energetically heaving her arse, muttering, panting, biting and generally being a noteworthy addition to the galaxy of great screws ... well ... then ... for all intents and purposes ...

An ESB Clerical Officer is totally blind.

Deaf and dumb too. Generally senseless, in fact. Because, you see, in such a situation ... lying on top of a young one who is energetically heaving her etcetera ... in such a situation an ESB Clerical Officer, much like the next man, he's concentrating on the business to hand. All his energies, all his receptive senses so to speak, all is devoted totally to extracting the maximum amount of sensation out of the young one's mucous membranes and, as a corollary, to inserting the maximum possible length of male member into her innards.

Thereby proving his manhood. Or something.

Enough said. I feel I've made my point.

I was blind to the outside world. Which, in so far as I could see, was totally dark anyway. Except for little flickers of light in Emily Farrell's eyes as she grinned at me.

I like a girl who grins. (It's your serious women who bring on the droop. Knew a serious woman once who ... oh never mind ... the past is another country and besides the wench is happily married in the suburbs.)

I like a girl who grins. And I liked Emily Farrell very much indeed. Her buttocks fitted my hands, so to speak ... her skinny little body felt RIGHT underneath my beer belly. Like Mutt and Jeff, Starsky and Hutch, Conor Cruise and O'Brien, we were made for each other.

THIS THING WAS BIGGER THAN BOTH OF US.
But then?
What happened then?
Well I'll tell you what happened then. Just when . . . precisely when Emily Farrell was five seconds away from orgasm and complete satisfaction, (naturally, naturally), precisely at that moment when she was saying "Achaggle ccchhhg" . . . well not really SAYING it . . . but those gurgling noises were coming from her throat, I was thrusting the last millimetre (went metric in '76) . . . the last millimetre of my member up into her to encourage this "achaggle ccchhhg" noise which I found very attractive. At the time. In retrospect it seems ridiculous. But anyhow. To the point. Precisely at the moment when Emily was . . .

I heard a voice. Over my head.

'What's going on here?'

Now the answer to that question, I felt at the time, still do as a matter of fact, still feel that that's the sort of question that even the participants on "Stop The Lights Quiz Show" could have answered with only a little help from Bunny Carr, the quiz master.

So I ignored it.

After all, Emily was only two seconds away from complete carnal satisfaction . . .

Her needs were greater than those of the foolish questioner.

I felt. Then I felt a hand, slapping me on the right buttock.

'Hey', said the voice that belonged to the hand. 'Hey I said what's going on here?'

I ignored that too. The man was obviously retarded.

One more MIGHTY THRUST . . .

AND THE DEED WAS DONE.

Emily screeched. Her body went into spasms as of epilepsy or some new dance craze. So violent, these spasms, that I was forced to disengage. We became two people again. I, standing up vaguely. Emily rolling about the grass, giggling, twitching and generally behaving in a peculiar manner.

'What's going on here', the questioner questioned again.

I looked at him, at Emily, back to him. Answers seemed superfluous. So I said nothing. I mean to say . . . damn it all . . . here I am . . . my trousers around my knees . . . and here's Emily sensuously stretching her limbs and rolling about the place, rubbing her pubes against a tuft of grass . . .

RUBBING HER PUBES AGAINST A TUFT OF GRASS?

This was going A BIT TOO FAR. I decided. My fatherly instincts reasserted themselves and I went to her, helped her to her feet, generally calmed the child down, helped her into her clothes, placing my body protectively between her nakedness and the eyes of the mad questioner.

That done, my arm about her shoulder, I turned to face him.

He was a policeman. Not only that, he was a sergeant of policemen, big and bulky, his stripes gleaming silver in the moonlight . . . AND NOT ONLY THAT . . . behind him, like altar boys at a concelebrated mass, behind him stood a semi-circle of others, not policemen, just others . . .

I looked at them carefully.

There were eight in all. Five of them were wearing strange black uniforms reminiscent of Roumanian traffic policemen. Some signal in my brain, some memory jiggled . . . and I realised that these were members of the Civil Defence . . . Jesus wept . . . I looked towards Dublin, expecting to see the fiery aftermath of the nuclear holocaust. But Dublin was still there. Intact.

So what was going on?

I examined the rest of the sergeant's posse. The last three were civilians in long socks, carrying small rucksacks, lights, ropes, axes, first aid kits, demountable stretchers, cooking equipment and for all I knew a portable Mater Misericordiae Hospital in their hip pockets.

These maniacs, I judged, these were Mountain Rescue.

But who were they rescuing? And what the hell was going on?

'What the hell is going on?' I asked.

'That's what I want to know', the policeman said, looking at me from the crook of his arm where his face was muttering into a walkie-talkie.

Who was he walkie-talkie-ing to?

I looked about. Sure enough, far down the mountain, across the bog . . . in actual fact right near where my car was parked, I saw three blue flashing lights.

OFFICIAL VEHICLES . . . DA . . . DUMMM.

The policeman, his conversation finished, approached. He looked at us cunningly, at Emily particularly. Sherlock Holmes, solving the Case of The Hound Of The Baservilles, he must have had an expression akin to this. Smug, perhaps the apposite word.

'Would your name, Miss, by any chance, be Emily Farrell?'

'No', she replied. 'My name is Martha Cunningham.'

I looked down at her in surprise. She looked up at me, her face all bland innocence, as if to say "didn't you know that was my name?"

'Aha', said the policeman. 'I have reason to believe . . .' He tapped his walkie-talkie, 'GOOD reason to believe that you are Emily farrell, aged fifteen-and-a-half, of Coolock. And THAT at this moment in time the harbour in Howth is being dragged for your body at considerable public expense not to say inconvenience to the members of the sub-aqua club.'

'Rubbish', said Emily Farrell of Coolock, whose body they were at that moment looking for in Howth. 'Rubbish, my name is Martha Cunningham. I am eighteen-and-a-half years old and a student at Rathmines College of Journalism where I hope to specialise in police brutality.'

I looked down at her in some admiration. She squeezed my hand. I squeezed hers in reciprocation.

'Aha', said the sergeant. 'Aha, Emily, you can't fool me. I happen to know . . .' Again, he tapped his walkie-talkie, as if within its plastic case there throbbed the HEART OF KNOWLEDGE . . . 'I happen to know that this morning YOU, EMILY FARRELL, you left your parents' home and ran away, behind you only a note which signified that you were about to hurl yourself into Howth harbour on account of John Travolta not replying to your fan letters.'

'Nonsense', said Emily, looking up at me for guidance.

Of which I had little to offer.

'I suppose he got you up to it', the sergeant said to her, referring, obviously, to me. 'An older man, it's always the way. Married, I'd say. Shocking. State. Of affairs.'

'No I got him up to it', said Emily suddenly. 'It's all my fault I confess I confess . . .' At which she fell to her knees and bowed elaborately, making mock-obeisance to the startled sergeant.

'Now let's not have a scene, miss', he suggested.

'My fault, my fault, woe is me', responded Emily.

'What the hell are you doing up this mountain anyway?

said I. 'Shouldn't you be looking for armed robbers who are a threat to the very fabric of the state?'

'Lights,' he said, 'we had reports of lights. Shooting off in all directions. Some said they were UFOs. Others thought it might be a crashed plane. These things have to be investigated. Now are you going to come quietly?'

'I'm not a UFO . . .', I protested, looking into the sky and wondering if I should mention to the sergeant that the lights folk had seen were merely the shades of Patrick Pearse and Deirdre of the Sorrows going back to The Beyond. Should I tell him that?

Perhaps not. Not just at this moment.

'Are you going to come quietly?' he repeated.

'Oh Martin', said Emily, hugging herself to my knees. 'You're being arrested, isn't it sad?'

'Come for what?' I asked. 'What have I done? Can a man not go up a mountain with his girlfriend?'

'Oh Martin,' said Emily, 'that's a lovely thing to say.'

'Thank you, Emily', I responded, bowing slightly in my courtly manner.

She looked at me with eyes aglow with love. 'Do you know something, Martin?' she said.

'What's that, my dear?' I replied.

'You've made a woman of me.' She nodded wisely. 'You'll get your reward for that.'

And she was right.

22

I GOT NINE months. Less remission for good behaviour let's say two months plus six months already served . . . two and six that equals eight . . . take eight away from nine . . . leaves one. That's four weeks.

In four weeks I'll be out.

In four weeks I'll have paid my debt to society for all those nasty sounding things I'm supposed to have done. Like carnal knowledge of a female minor. That's a nasty one. That one lost me my job in the ESB. A man can do a lot of things and still remain a Clerical Officer in Head Office. But carnal knowledge of a female minor has you out through the front doors quicker than you can say 'pension rights'.

And as for 'Indecent Assault'. Well. That doesn't help either. Indecent assault lost me my position of trust in the Residents' Association. I mean to say . . . they wrote to me . . . I mean to say Martin old chap we all have young daughters here in Glenageary and you know the way it is have you tried to get medical attention?

They can do wonders these days. With hormones.

No. Whatever way you look at it. My fellow residents weren't too keen on indecent assault. Not that it pleased me much either.

It sounds so sort of scruffy. IN DECENT assault. Yik. So lacking in je ne sais quoi. Esprit du Corps. Elan. Après tous, je suis un homme d'affaires et ce n'est pas possible pour moi . . .

Indecent assault always brings to mind those pale-eyed chaps with raincoats and domineering mothers. Chaps who leap out of hedges to bite the firm white thighs white thighs white thighs of gym-slipped schoolgirls CHOMP.

Not that I would mind THAT.

We're all HUMAN.

BUT . . . the running away bit would get me. The leaving of one's dentures solidly embedded in the firm young flesh the firm young flesh the

FIRM

YOUNG

FLESH

That would really BUG me. Particularly when the cops arrive on one's doorsteps with the dentures as Exhibit A in a plastic bag, eerily recalling in one's mind those half-forgotten pantos in the Gaiety with Maureen Potter when Prince Charming went from door to door with Cinderella's slipper.

'Would you mind slipping these teeth into your gob for a moment, MISTER O'Shea?'

Dear Mother of God.

Sex will be the death of me.

As it very nearly was. On the morning of My Case.

On the morning of My Case I stood on the steps of the courts in Chancery Place, reflecting on the transient nature of freedom when one is out on bail and watching people pass. Strange, I mused, strange how in Places like Chancery Place all the passers-by seem to be either policemen or lawyers or criminals. One watches them, trying to tell one from t'other. Sometimes it's not easy but maybe . . .

Maybe these are just ordinary folks. Maybe the ambience of the environment flows over the passing citizenry, reflecting itself on them. Like the sun sometimes reflecting itself on the Grand Canal Basin beside the gasworks at Ringsend sometimes makes it appear as a pool in which Yeats might see swans . . . Like how on dark evenings further up that very same canal all the women wandering seem to be prostitutes, ban-gardai . . . or members of The Legion of Mary . . . and maybe they are

Sometimes it is not easy to tell a lady's Profession.

So. I stood on the steps of the court. In Wordsworthian Mood. Things flashing upon my inward eye. Which is the bliss of solitude. Yes. I was alone and I smoked my last cigarette before going in to surrender myself to Justice which, being blind, would no doubt condemn me. After I'd helped it across the road.

I was alone. Anna had gone in to get a good seat in the public gallery. Where, no doubt, she would giggle, somehow having decided that the whole affair was highly amusing. Emily Farrell, the meantime, was somewhere else, hopefully learning the lines which I'd instructed her to say in the witness box. I was alone
UNTIL . . .
A small man about five foot six inches high in a blue suit the colour of the sky came up the steps. He carried himself jauntily, indeed cockily, a halo of self-imposed importance hovering about his person like the exhaust from a badly tuned diesel lorry going up Temple Hill in Blackrock at five o'clock to the outrage of environmentally-minded commuters.

I looked at him.

The five pens in his top pocket brought to mind a former leader of the Labour Party whose retirement the country was now enjoying. Brought to mind . . . yes . . . but this man was not the former leader of the Labour Party.

Not yet.

Instinctively I knew who he was. But tried not to think about it. Instead, as he approached, I ruminated about those pens in his top pocket, those almost witchdoctor symbols with which he no doubt impressed the semi-literate readers of the Daily Mirror who were his followers. Are they real, I thought, those pens? Or merely symbols? And if they are that latter, then are they constructed in a manner reminiscent of those false handkerchiefs of yore which were two-thirds cardboard and were given out free by the better class of dry-cleaning establishment when the customer counted — And not just his change.

Are they real, those pens?

Yes. They are real. I had read what they write.

Reports of sub-committees. Manifestos various. Statements, both of policy and position. Outline synopses of the inherent factors involved. Definitive analyses of hitherto unquantified problems inherent in structures. On behalf of. Ad hoc. De Jure. Trocaire.

Rights of. Workers. Imperialism. Entrenched clauses
Entrenched coats. Nonsense.
Bitterness
Loch Ness
Monster

Of hate.

Yes. I knew this man . . . trade union functionary . . . corporal of the corporate state, his union rulebook under his armpit like a Mormon's bible or a gambler's derringer, any dispute to be solved by whipping it out and blasting it away at his opponent. I knew him well. Emily Farrell's father.

He stopped beside me.

'O'Shea?', he inquired.

I looked at him blandly. 'I don't think I've had the pleasure', I mentioned politely.

'Oh you've had that alright,' he smirked, 'and now you're going to pay for it.' He looked up at me. 'You little bastard', he added. Inappropriately, I felt, in view of our relative heights. 'You little bastard. I'm Emily's father.'

'Well eh . . .'

I said. Nothing else came to mind. Only to wonder at the magnificence of God's Plan, at how, through some genetic abberation, how this creep had fathered the lithe and lissom, lovely little Emily.

'It's cunts like you,' he said, 'cunts like you this country can do without.'

'Well eh . . .'

I said. Wondering which particular type of cunt the country could well do with.

He looked me up and down contemptuously, perhaps in the same manner that the guards in the Gulag must've looked at Alexander Solzhenitsyn . . . a noble man with whom I feel a certain affinity.

Mr Farrell looked me up and down contemptuously. And, after a pause, in itself contemptuous too, he said:

'B L O O D S U C K E R'

So. I decided that it was time now to stop saying 'well eh', suitable as it was in the circumstances, time to put my oar in.

'I pay tax too.'

'Don't be smart with me.' He waved a fist in front of my nose. 'For two pins . . . TWO pins.'

'Well I can understand your feelings', I retreated slightly. 'I'm a father too.'

'Well you shouldn't be. You lot should be castrated. Like in

Germany.'

'What lot?'

'You lot. Child molesters.'

'Are you SURE they castrate them in Germany?' I asked, mentally altering certain vague plans for a holiday trip down the Rhine. Which was to be the year after the trip down the Shannon, the wife-swapping trip as previously mentioned with My Friend Walter. 'Are you SURE? Damn it all . . . Germany's in the Common Market . . . I'm sure the bureaucrats in Brussels would have a thing to say about castration. They have a say about most things. Like what grade a carrot is. Or the specific gravity of beer. Or the . . .'

'I'm not going to bandy words with you.' Farrell held up the palm of his right hand. 'I've met your sort. Don't think I haven't. All piss and wind and fancy accents. Well two can play at that game. Your day is done. Mark my words. Washed up.' He looked about scornfully at the architectural magnificence of the Four Courts, the well cut stone, the elegant neo-classical proportions of the edifice, the bullet holes from some fracas or other, the neat piles of dogshit dotting the ground in intricate and almost Byzantine patterns which, like dots on a Miro painting, belonged there, in that position . . . and nowhere else.

'Revolutionary courts', he roared, 'revolutionary courts . . . That's where it's at. No hanging about. To hell with these outmoded institutions of oppression. Only serve to give jobs to a lot of lawyers and bumboys. Drinking brandy and old wines in there while the masses starve. To hell with them. The needs of the people must come before the privilege of the few. The establishment must be swept aside. The judges must be judged. The day is coming. Mark my words. I see it now. The people are on the march. Their cause is just. Neither tanks nor guns nor fancy words will stop them. Revolutionary is an ongoing situation. The blood of the few must be spilled for the good of the many. No more shilly-shallying around. The pictures in the National Gallery are better housed than the people of this city. What am I talking about? The DOGS of the rich in Foxrock are better fed than the children of the poor. Connolly was right. Marx was right. Lenin was right. The left is right. Power comes out of the barrel of a gun. The rulers won't listen to reason. Look at Cuba. I'm not saying it's perfect. No human institution is perfect. But we can only try. We must build anew. And to build we must first destroy. Everyone knows that. Even property speculators know that. Look at this city. Look around you. Think. Is this what Wolfe Tone died for? Is this what Emmet died for? Is this what Connolly was carried out, a wounded man, a wounded man, carried out to die for? Is this what generations of Irishmen, and Irishwomen, we are all brothers, to our sisters, the oppression of women is another side to the same coin make no mistake. All shall be equal in the workers' republic. No man shall dine in splendour while his brother starves. Remember what Yeats said. And O'Casey. He knew. And what was his reward? I'll tell you what his reward was. Driven out. HOUNDED out. Of his own country. Why? I'll tell you why. Because he dared to speak the truth. Well I'm not afraid to speak the truth. As long as there's breath in my body. I'll not be hounded out. I'll not be bought off. I have my pride. You can take everything from a man. But you can't take away his pride. You can oppress him with poverty. But you can't . . . LOOK AT the injustice. For them that have eyes. A nod is as good as a wink. Look at the injustice. There's people in this city oh you may mock. There's people in this city who have to watch over their children at night for fear of the rats. For fear of the rats. While the children of the rich are getting bandy legged up on horses in Howth. Is that right? No. That is NOT right. Is that Christian? No that is not Christian. Is this a Christian country? No it is not a Christian country. The pagans in the Congo . . . the niggers in the trees out there are more Christian than the people in this country. The priests in this country are on the side of the oppressors. Always have been. Must be swept aside. What do they know of hunger? Have they ever seen their children starve? No. They have not. They've made their bed. Must lie on it. It's too late. Enemies of the people everywhere . . .'

'Swept ASIDE.' He waved his arm magnificently, bringing to mind a garden gnome manufactured in the likeness of James Larkin addressing the striking ranks of United Tramways Workers in nineteen thirteen. 'Swept ASIDE, this THIS . . . these institutions to suppress the masses . . .'

'Well it's ME they're suppressing right now.'

He ignored me. In full flight, his eyes alight, his pens clicking together with rage, he continued, myself and two ban-gardai at the bottom of the steps looking up at him nervously.

'I'm not an enemy of the people', I put in meekly.

He ignored me, absorbing my remark into his tirade. 'Living off their backs. Seducing the innocent daughters of the workers.'

'Emily's not an innocent daughter of the workers.'

He stopped, his eyes narrowing. His mouth narrowing. His nose too, strangely, narrowing. Every feature narrowing so that he looked . . . like a ferret. Not that I've ever SEEN a ferret. But I somehow think I know what a ferret looks like. And so, in a peculiar manner, my relationship with ferrets is somewhat akin to my relationship with God.

People keep ferrets. In England. In their back gardens. Particularly in the working class areas of Yorkshire. Where they keep pigeons too. To race against each other. They use the ferrets to catch rabbits. Though I have heard that there is a sport which involves the putting of ferrets down one's trouser legs. As a sort of virility test. Though it would strike one as likely to perform an opposite function. However . . . ferrets certainly remind one that the English are a strange people and that perhaps Patrick Pearse was right to break the link. To be ruled by a country of ferret fanciers is an ignominious state of affairs for a proud and ancient race.

But enough of politics . . .

Enough to say that Farrell looked at me with narrowed eyes.

'Aha . . . so that's your angle is it?'

'What?'

'You've got some fancy lawyer in there who's going to make out Emily as some kind of whore. Blacken her name. That's it, is it?'

'Not at all. Emily is, in my opinion, a very fine young woman. And, as a matter of fact, I don't have a laywer. I'm defending myself.'

'Good', said Farrell looking at me cunningly. 'That should be worth another six months.'

'I pay for my mistakes', I intoned in a noble manner perhaps reminiscent of Robert Emmet or Lord Edward Fitzgerald or some other superior class of citizen about to offer up the supreme sacrifice, knowing full well that history would be the judge. 'I pay for my mistakes. Like a gentleman.'

Farrell, the word 'gentleman' obviously even less acceptable to him than the word 'Shah' to the Ayatollah, Farrell made gobbling motions with his throat muscles and spat on the ground. The spit landed very close to my Italian slip-ons. I stared down at it, fascinated as ever at how members of the working classes are able to produce these globules of yellow phlegm at will.

'Gentleman my arse', roared Farrell, suddenly, catching me unawares, giving me a hefty push. Affronted by being taken aback like this I prepared to retaliate but, losing my balance, I toppled backwards down the steps. And that is how sex was nearly the death of me. However, I was saved by the two lady policemen still standing there at the bottom of the steps, landing comfortably in their arms, their mighty serge-clad bosoms cradling my head in an agreeable manner.

'Bollicks', shouted Farrell down at me, turned about and went into the courthouse.

The ban-gardai, no better girls, hefted me to my feet, happy grins on their nice plain Castlebar faces. I thanked them profusely and followed Farrell into the courthouse. I walked down echoing corridors. And in my mind a question . . . do ban-gardai or don't they . . . late at night in the barracks with the lads? But the polished halls of justice held no answers

Only another question

What the hell am I doing here?

23

THE COURT SAT and I stood. The charges were read out. Gasps from old bags in the public gallery with nothing better to do than sit here and wait for Children's Allowance Day. Gasps and mutterings and a continuous nattering as of women everywhere when their betters are about to get their come-uppance.

Damn the bird-eyed old crones anyway, I thought, may their dugs wither . . . may their husbands come home drunk and beat the shit out of them . . . may the battered wives hostel be full up when they arrive on the doorstep with their mewling brats hanging out of their varicose veins . . . may the Corpo relocate them to a tower block in Ballymun . . .

And may the lifts be broken down . . .

That's what I thought. But what I said was a different matter entirely.

'Ah come on now judge have a heart. How do you mean "indecent assault"? I mean to say we're both men of the world.'

A slow smile, not overly loaded with mirth, drifted across his features. I knew instinctively that he was thinking of his half-finished Irish Times crossword which he'd had to leave in a quiet leatherbound corner of the Law Library, thinking of his abandoned glass of Madeira, the letter from the Taoiseach BEGGING him to volunteer for the Special Criminal Court . . . the little things that make a judge's life worthwhile. He'd had to leave all that. To deal with me.

'I'm afraid, Mr O'Shea,' he remarked to assorted legal titters, 'I'm afraid that your world and mine seem to have very little in common.'

'Oh granted,' I admitted, 'but INDECENT ASSAULT? I mean that's a bit MUCH, wouldn't you say? I mean that sounds like rape or something REALLY nasty.'

'Well,' the judge announced, 'as a layman you may misinterpret the term. It's merely a technical charge.'

'That's OK,' says me, quick as a flash, 'as long as I'll go to a technical jail for it.'

'No. You'll go to a real jail.'

The judge smiled, paused to allow the assembled gentlemen of the press time to write down his quips, smiled again, then looked seriously down at me.

'Mr O'Shea . . .' He announced gravely. 'Mr O'Shea you have pleaded guilty to the extremely serious charges as set out here before me. The only mitigating factor I can find is that you have pleaded guilty, thereby saving the unfortunate young lady involved the trauma of having to appear in the witness box.'

I looked around the courtroom. The unfortunate young lady involved, sitting in the visitor's gallery, waved enthusiastically at me. I smiled back at her.

'Mr O'Shea . . . perhaps I might have your attention. For a moment?'

'Sorry Judge.'

'As I was saying. That is the only mitigating factor. I will admit, however, that having heard Sergeant Mulhall's evidence I had at first grave doubts as to your fitness to stand trial.'

'You mean you thought I was bananas?'

'Precisely. Though "bananas" is not, in a strictly legal sense, the absolutely apposite word.'

(Absolutely apposite hilarity from the assembled legal chaps.)

'Silence please.' The judge held up his hand in the manner of a comedian stifling the applause, as if to say if you think that's funny well this'll make you wet yourselves.

'Silence please. This is a court of law. As I was saying, Mr O'Shea, you will recall that the psychiatric advisors to the prison service have adjudged you fit to stand trial. Not for me to quibble with their judgement. Though I must admit that your story of Patrick Pearse and Deirdre of the Sorrows is, in my opinion, the most absurd and scurrilous fabrication that I have heard in a lifetime on the bench. It ILL BEHOVES you, Mr O'Shea, ill behoves you, when we have only recently celebrated the centenary of the birth of that outstanding patriot, ill-behoves you to bring, dare I say DRAG, to drag his much beloved name into this case. Not only that, to suggest, to imply that in some way the ghost of the beloved patriot incited you to make love to an innocent child who . . . absurdity piled upon absurdity . . . an innocent child who was, as you allege, in actual fact, Deirdre of the Sorrows.'

'Well I wouldn't put it quite like that.'

'How WOULD you put it, Mr O'Shea?'

'Well I'm not quite sure how I would put it. But I wouldn't put it quite like that. In any case she's not an innocent child.'

'How do you mean I'm not an innocent child?', this from Emily Farrell in a shriek from the back of the court.

I turned around.

'You started it', I shouted up at her.

'Silence in court', said the judge.

At which a flip-flop sandal sailed through the air in an arc and landed with a plop in front of the judge . . . he looked at it solemnly. 'Bring that girl before the court,' he murmured ominously.

They brought her.

'Did you throw that sandal?'

'Yes judge', said Emily.

'Why, may I ask?'

''Cos I'm pissed off with all this crap.'

'These proceedings,' the judge intoned, 'are for your protection. Whether you like it or not. The State has a duty to protect its young girls from degenerates.'

'I'm not the State's young girls,' riposted Emily, 'I'm me.'

The judge, suddenly, looked very very tired. Very very tired indeed. I almost felt sorry for him. But not quite. After all, he'd just called me a degenerate.

'Now listen, little girl . . . you go back up there to your seat and not a peep out of you or I'll hold you in contempt.'

'What does that mean when you're at home?'

'It means that you will be LOCKED UP.'

'Oh.'

Emily retreated.

My case went on. Or, rather, my judge went on. My case was over. This was his verdict.

'As I was saying, Mr O'Shea, mitigating factors. None. I have taken into account your young wife's testimony that you have always been a dutiful husband, a faithful provider and a model citizen and father. You are lucky to have such a wife.'

I looked around. The wife I was lucky to have waved at me, a big grin on her face and Aoife on her knee. Aoife waved too.

145

I began to feel that no-one, apart from me, no-one was taking this seriously. Why would they? It was me that was going to be locked up.

'I sentence you to nine months.'

'Thank you, Judge.'

And I was led away. Through corridors dank, past clanging doors, the smell of piss and the sound of muffled traffic, waiting on the quay for traffic lights

which would not change for me.

But ah . . . aha I thought, stone walls do not a prison make, nor iron bars a cage . . .

* * *

And I was wrong.

They do.

But no matter. I have now only four weeks left to serve. I can look on the bright side. Anna has managed OK in the outside world. She's got a job with an order of enclosed nuns. As all the nuns are over eighty and do not understand the modern world, Anna was hired by their trustees to look after the poor old dears. No better girl. She'll make their last days comfortable. Soon they'll all be dead. And the trustees will sell the convent lands to speculative builders. Neo-Georgian houses, close together (but detached), will sprout. Housewives will go mad where once the quiet nuns would walk in quiet prayer. Time marches on.

And the world changes.

Anna's job is nine to five but, ever resourceful, she's hired an au pair to look after little Aoife. And the au pair's name is Emily Farrell. They became friendly during the courtcase. And, some weeks after my unfortunate incarceration, Emily had severe disagreements with her parents, packed her bags and left, straggling across the city like a waif to the motherly Anna. Every third visiting day, Emily comes to see me in the prison, cheering me up with her childish beauty . . . innocent ways.

And, on the other available days, Anna comes in with her latest laughter, latest sorrow . . . to confide in me. She sits across the visiting table and I notice the warders who hover nearby looking at her big breasts and don't blame them. And I look too.

Breasts are few
And far between
In Mountjoy Jail.
And so and so. All's well on the home front.

Which is just as well. A man needs a stable family background. My new cellmate, that was his problem. Or so he says. He didn't have a stable family background. That's why he sawed up his sweetheart and posted her feet to the Duke of Edinburgh.

He was unhinged. Due to the lack of a stable family background.

'But why the Duke of Edinburgh' I asked the lunatic.

'Political, isn't it?' he said, political.'

I agreed. I always agree with people who are prone to sawing up their fellow citizens. Particularly when I have to share my sleeping accommodation with them.

It's unnerving.

The nights are long. I do not sleep. My cellmate is on the blanket for political status. He sits there naked, wrapped in his grey blanket, staring at the wall.

I do not like it.

I stare at him.

Four weeks is a long time to stay awake. But I look on the bright side. It is March and soon it will be April. The birds are singing in the trees along Iona Road. I hear the trains on the railway line that passes between Mountjoy and that same Iona Road.

Soon I will be free.

And then perhaps I will sing like a bird in a tree. Or travel in a train along a railway line, perhaps. Perhaps not. The only certainty is that I do not know . . . where precisely I will go . . . if anywhere at all.

So perhaps I will go home.

That seems a good idea.

At home I have a wife to love. And a child to watch. And a bone to pick with Deirdre of the Sorrows.